Shadow's Flight

A Fighter Pilot's Story

GREGORY DEAN TAYLOR

A Place In Time.Press • Beverly Hills, CA

DEDICATIONS

GREATEST GENERATION INSPIRATION

Lt. Col Murray and Vera Taylor & Colonel Charles and Leona Dye

NEXT GENERATION INSPIRATION

Ty, Samantha, Luke, Lauren, Courtney, Jalen, Tiphanie, Jasmine & Micah

SIBLING SUPPORT TEAM

Cheryl, Scott, & Todd

SPECIAL DEDICATION – SUSAN TAYLOR!

Without her heartfelt support, this story would not have happened

SPECIAL THANKS

Elene, Rachael, Steve, De, & Fleet for helping turn this book dream into a reality.

Fleet Lentz (Fleet), Robert Panico (Dog Breath) & Terry Gleason (Casino) for adding their personal tales to this book

To the Pilots, RIOs & WSOs that created the Fighter Pilot world this book describes and that I so enjoyed!

To those Marines & Airmen that took great pride in making sure my Phantom always brought me safely home!

A Place in Time.Press
8594 Wilshire Blvd. Ste. 1020,
Beverly Hills, CA 90211
310 613-8872

e-mail: info@aplaceintime.press
Website: aplaceintime.press

Cover Design, Layout, Edits: Christopher Staser, brandweaver.tv
Illustration: Michael Xavier

Library of Congress Cataloging-in-Publication Data is available on file.

Print ISBN: 978-0-9745414-6-4
Ebook ISBN: 978-0-9745414-7-1

Historical Fiction

Printed in the United States of America

Our books may be purchased in bulk for promotional, educational, or business use. Please contact your local bookseller or the publisher.

First U.S. Edition 2022

PREFACE

During the 1970's and 1980's I had the privilege to fly the McDonnell Douglas F-4 Phantom Jet for over eighteen years accumulating close to three thousand flight hours. This book is my attempt to share the story of my experience with this magnificent aircraft and more importantly, introduce the men who shared these experiences with me.

Those two decades were a glorious period when wild and non-politically correct actions and antics were still allowed in the military. This was a time when only men were allowed to fly fighter aircraft, therefore my adventures and escapades feature only men/warriors that were fortunate enough to fly the Phantom or support the Phantom. All were volunteers and most were college graduates. Many joined when being in the military was not popular. They served their country and some died doing it. They loved flying the Phantom and they loved the squadron life.

The F-4 Phantom entered service with the U.S Navy in 1961. At that time it was the Navy's fastest, highest flying and longest range fighter. It had climbed to 98,556 feet and set the world's speed record at 1,604 miles per hour (over two times the speed of sound). It was later introduced into the United States Air Force and eventually eleven other countries. I had the opportunity to fly the F-4 Models B, J, N, S and E.

The Phantom served both the Navy Blue Angels and Air Force Thunderbirds demonstration teams. It saw combat in Viet Nam and Operation Desert Storm. It was big, fast, and loud. It looked mean with huge air intakes and afterburners. It featured wings at swept up to the sky and a stabilator that swooped down ...s the ground. It looked dangerous, and it was. It had un... r, like a street dragster, that saved it time and again.

... y story based only on my faulty memory and ... mine. It includes personal tales from some of the Pilots and RIO's that flew with me and they allowed me to add them to this book. During my years of flying I encountered hundreds of aircrew but in this book I have only used aviator Call Signs, not real names. On occasion I have made up a call sign to protect the guilty.

Surrounding and supporting the aircrew were families, friends and especially wives and kids. They provided love and support when the aircrew was overseas in combat, deployed or just flying with the USMC Reserves. They changed homes and schools wherever they were asked and they found work and raised their children often times without much help. My wife and I moved fifteen times during my flying career and raised two children. So although this book does not center on the family it is important to know that family involvement featuring both enjoyment and pain were always part of the story.

Writing this history has allowed me to relive in my mind things that I lived through fifty years ago. The chance to collect the adventures and escapades and revisit my old friends from the past has been extremely valuable to me. It was like I got to experience those great times one more time. Truly I feel it was a great run of fighter squadron life, exciting flights, memorable screw ups, outlandish fun, tragic deaths and inspired leadership.

I take pride in having made great friends while serving America and I will always be thankful for the opportunity I had to fly the McDonnell Douglas F-4 Phantom, one of the finest fighter aircraft ever built. I hope you enjoy this tale and always remember the wisdom passed on to me – **Always Pursue Targets of Opportunity** and **Speed Is Life!**

SHADOW'S FLIGHT

A FIGHTER PILOT'S STORY

TABLE OF CONTENTS

FORWARD

It was 2011, San Diego, California. It was to be a reunion of U.S. Marine Corps F-4 Phantom fighter pilots and RIOs. I had flown my last Phantom flight in 1988. Twenty three years before and yet it felt like yesterday. I was now in my early sixty's. As I pulled into the parking lot I was excited but anxious. Would I recognize anybody? Would anybody recognize or remember me? I headed into the area that had been designated the Reunion Ready Room.

I walked in and looked around. Who were all these old guys? Some had long hair, many had little hair. A few were sporting full beards, some overweight and nobody looked like anyone I remembered. I went to the sign-in table and got my Name Tag: Greg Taylor – SHADOW. I looked around for someone I might recognize. As I scanned the room a transformation began to happen. I did recognize some of these old guys. Somebody yelled "SHADOW" and waved me over! We started to shake hands, hug and pound each other on the back. We began to share personal updates. Soon old stories, adventures and escapades started to be shared. We couldn't stop smiling.

I was back among my brothers. I talked with Milo, Grunt, Mambel, Rookie, Gene, Jumper, Spider, Dog Breath, Fleet, HJ, Casino, Snoopy, Eagle, Watchdog, Woody, Frisco, Smiley, Crazy, Z-Man, Stick, Killer, Pig, Dog and at least fifty more. Then I saw an older man, a bit hunched over, a little hair, but totally surrounded by guys crowding around him and laughing. His grin, smile and sparkling eyes were unchanged. He started to tell another story and everyone nodded and laughed. It was Lancer. To most of us he represented Marine Corps flying and the Phantom. He was the most inspirational leader most of us had ever known, in or out of the Corps. I knew he had impacted my flying career more than any other Marine.

I wandered over, feeling a little hesitant. Would he recognize or remember me? He looked up, saw me, and that big grin appeared as he stuck out his hand and said "Hey Shadow!"... I was home.

That Phantom Reunion is when I decided I had to tell my story. Perhaps my individual story is nothing special, but I had twenty years of flying fighters. I had an unusual flying career having flown for two decades earning both Navy and Air Force Wings. During that time I had amassed close to three thousand hours flying the F-4 Phantom and flew close to two hundred combat missions. I experienced adventures, escapades and incidents both in the air and on the ground that one just could not make up.

The tales which I am going to share with you are as true as I and others remember them. The adventures and escapades were sometimes exciting, often dangerous, and occasionally wild. We took pride in being professionals but never let that interfere with our success and fun. I feel compelled to tell these tales not because of my flying, but rather because of the crazy cast of characters with whom I shared these adventures. Earlier I listed some of the Call Signs of the aviators I saw at the reunion. In the chapters that follow I will introduce you to a few of these flyers, jokers, friends, clowns, heroes and legends. I had the privilege to spend time with these men in the 1970s and 80's. I was a younger man then, living in a Fighter Pilot's world, which will likely never be replicated! Welcome aboard, I hope you enjoy the flight!

PART ONE

How I Became a Marine and a Pilot

CHAPTER ONE

CREATING A MARINE

When I was a young boy I always assumed I would become a pilot. My father, Murray Taylor, had been a B-29 Super Fortress Bomber pilot in World War II. He had flown combat missions over Japan and had also served during the Korean War. He ended up as a Lt. Colonel in the U.S Air Force Reserve. In addition, my Uncle, Charles Dye, had been a Belly Gunner in a B-24 Liberator flying missions over Germany. He had been shot down over France and served two years as a German POW. He stayed active in the Air Force and later became a Colonel and served around the world. Like most Combat veterans, neither my father nor my uncle spoke about their combat experiences. Occasionally they might share a little story, typically something funny, but never about the real grim missions that they had flown. Even so, it was obvious they took great pride in the fact they had served. To my regret I never pushed them to tell me about their time flying.

My path was not so straight forward. It was 1968 and the Viet Nam War was still going strong but was not popular particularly among many college students. The world was in turmoil. Martin Luther King and Robert Kennedy had been assassinated. The Democratic convention in Chicago had spun out of control. Recreational drugs were growing and race relations were tense. The president, LBJ, was struggling with Viet Nam and in Viet Nam the Tet Offensive had just begun. Student Protests were occurring and the hippy movement and free love were still popular. Long hair was prevalent on college campuses.

Meanwhile, I was going to Washington State University in Pullman, Washington. I was planning to graduate with a Teaching degree with a focus on English and History. Things were a little slow in regard to world and national events but they were just starting to heat up at my University. I would be graduating in May and moving on.

It occurred to me when I was a senior that I should go talk to the Air Force Recruiter if I wanted to become a pilot. I was told that the Air Force had plenty of pilots and if I had wanted to be a pilot I should have talked with them when I was a freshman, and that perhaps I should have joined Air Force ROTC. That was a good point, but a little late. So I then talked with the local Navy Recruiter. I was told the Navy had plenty of pilots and if I had been interested in being a Navy pilot I should have perhaps joined the Naval ROTC years before. Another good point.

Then things took on some urgency. That spring I received a Notice in the mail and was told that I was to catch a bus early in the summer and go take my army physical. I then rode a bus into Seattle where I passed my Army physical along with two hundred other potential recruits. This was not looking good. My future was becoming not only murky, but not at all what I had dreamed. If I continued down this path I not only would not be a pilot but I likely wouldn't be an Officer... and I might be dead.

Right there on the spot I decided that if I was going to be a ground pounder, I would rather be a Marine. My deep thinking on this subject included the thought that they had a reputation for being tough and, well, I liked their uniforms. In addition to that, I figured girls would also be more attracted to me as a Marine. With that in mind I went to the U.S Marine Corps recruiting station in downtown Seattle. Upon entering the recruiting station I noticed they had photos of aircraft on the walls. I asked if the Marine Corps had aircraft and pilots and they said they certainly did, and if I was interested I could take an eye test and an Aviation Qualification test. They told me if I passed both of those tests I could sign an Aviation Contract. I passed both and signed a USMC Aviation Contract.

What that meant was that I would go to Quantico, Virginia in October and join a Marine Corps Officer Candidate Training Class (OCS). If I successfully passed that training course I would become a Marine Corps Officer. Then, I would be sent to Pensacola, Florida and enter into Naval Flight Training.

However, if I failed OCS in Quantico I would be relegated to Marine Corps Recruit Depot at Parris Island, South Carolina. Once training was completed in South Carolina, I would become a private in the Marine Corps, and would probably soon be assigned to combat in Viet Nam. Also, I learned that if I later failed flight school in Pensacola, I would no longer be a Marine pilot, but rather join the Marines as a ground officer. Both positions would mean serving in Viet Nam on the ground where life expectancy was not excellent. I signed the contract and became a member of the finest fighting force in the world:

MARINES The Few The Proud.

I have always been lucky!

I said goodbye to my family and my friends and jumped on a commercial aircraft bound for Quantico, Virginia. Like all new Marines, the first few days and weeks were extremely difficult. When we first got off the bus we had young men from all over the United States with long hair trying to stand at attention while the Drill Instructors roamed around us sharing their poor opinion of this class. The first day they marched us into a base barbershop where they shaved your head in under three minutes.

There was a lot of long hair on the floor when they were finished. We then had to run over to a building and get our boots and uniforms and foot lockers and we then ran stumbling with them to the barracks. We were then to get into our uniform and line up outside at attention. In under one hour they had completely changed the appearance of over fifty officer candidates.

We soon understood that the Corps doesn't care how rich or poor you are. They don't care where you went to school. They don't care about anything except how you perform right now. If they tell you to do fifty push-ups and you complete them they say "give me twenty five more." If you complete those, then they say "give me twenty five more." Finally you are struggling with your arms shaking.

"Give me one for your girlfriend", they shout. You give them one weak partial push up.

"Give me one for the Commandant!" they say while standing above you with a scowl on their face. You do a struggling half push up.

"Well can you at least give me one for the Marine Corps?"

At that point you can't get off the ground and just like every other officer candidate in the room you have failed. The Marine Drill Instructor begins telling you how worthless we all are as a platoon, and that we are the worst he has ever been given the miserable job of trying to turn into Marines.

My first day did not begin well. We were introduced to our Drill Instructor (DI), a combat experienced Sergeant. After our buzz haircuts and uniform fitting he lined us up for shots with medics on both sides shoving needles into each arm. I have always hated injections and soon I heard somebody moaning... and discovered it was me. I had fainted and was lying on my face on the cement floor. They dragged me into a small room and laid me down on a cot. My Drill Instructor came over and addressed me just two inches from my face.

"My Marine Corps didn't need pussy maggots like you!" and "I am going to see you don't make it!" he yelled in my ear.

Welcome aboard Greg! Things are looking bright.

We stayed in a large squad bay with bunk beds and each candidate had a stand up locker and a foot locker. The first morning the DI threw a metal garbage can down the middle of the Squad Bay at 5:30 to wake us up.

"You have five minutes to be properly dressed and standing at attention outside," he shouted.

Everything was like that. Almost impossible tasks with always a threat of being kicked out. The showers were gang showers, and we were given five minutes for over sixty Marines to make it through the shower. When we went on a platoon march we were never told if we were going for a mile march or fifteen miles. If the Platoon Leader started double timing we didn't know if it would last one hundred yards or two miles.

During our first weapons (rifle) inspection our DI felt that one candidate's weapon was unsatisfactory and he just turned and threw it into the nearby swamp. He then told the recruit to go get it, and that he had better never present his weapon to him again in that unclean condition.

We would be ordered to go outside and stand at attention and wait for our Platoon Leader Lieutenant. So we would run outside and snap to attention in the cold and we would just stand there five minutes, ten minutes, maybe fifteen minutes, at attention. What would go thru my mind was that I was not going to keep standing here. That this was ridiculous. That I'm not doing it. Fifteen minutes later the Platoon Leader would come out and we would all still be standing at attention.

We marched endlessly and were graded. We took academics tests and were graded. We took physical fitness tests and were graded. We competed in Leadership exercises and were graded. We worked in the Chow Hall. We shined boots. We climbed towers. We ran obstacle courses. When we went on the long runs over difficult terrain and someone began to drop out, the entire platoon would go back to the recruit who had stopped and we would run circles around that recruit until he got up and joined us again. If he didn't join us, then he would be put into the back of an ambulance and would be driven just in front of the running platoon so we could see him riding in comfort as we were marching or running behind the jeep. Candidates began to be kicked out and sent to Parris Island infantry training. We all succeeded or we all failed. I remember one difficult force march (extreme challenge exercise) over very hilly terrain. Although typically I did OK on these marches that day, I just didn't have it. We started up one hill and I decided I was going to lag back. One of the other candidates named Gene was jogging beside me, and saw what I was doing. He immediately grabbed my arm and started pulling me up the hill saying,

"No you don't!"

He wouldn't let me slow down or stop so I finally got a second wind and finished the trek. That lesson has always stayed with me that no matter who you are, at some time you are going to need someone to pull you through. Teamwork is everything.

Some people have the mistaken notion that individuals that are put in terrible situations in combat but will keep fighting and eventually risk death are doing it for their mission, or family or their nation. The truth is, the individual is doing it because if they don't their brother may die because they didn't do their job. That focus on teamwork and ultimate accountability to their peers is what drives their actions.

It was very interesting to experience this growth process. At first you hated the Drill Instructor. Gradually the hate turned into respect as we began to change and excel. When we finished we knew he had made us into Marines. We were all in shape. We were confident and gung ho about leading Marines in combat. It no longer mattered if you were from New York City or Tennessee. If you went to a community college or Notre Dame. If your family was wealthy or dirt poor. What mattered was that we were Marines for life.

I went into Quantico with a mission to excel. I had trained to be physically ready and worked hard to be the best. I could do more pull-ups than others and I was pretty fast. I could do the obstacle course faster than anyone in the Company. My Bunk Mate, Gene, became my best friend. He was from Detroit, Michigan, a little older than myself, and was also on an aviation contract. We worked and studied together to make sure we scored high in everything. At the end of the Officer Candidate school, I graduated as the Honor Man in our Platoon and was number two in the Company that was composed of three platoons. Gene had also done very well.

At that time we learned about a special program that was being put in place. If you had an Aviation Contract and graduated in the top 10% of your OCS class, you would be going to Air Force Flight Training rather than Naval Flight Training. If you graduated between 10% and 20%, you would be sent to the Army Flight School. All other Aviation Contract Officers were to go to Pensacola and the Naval Flight School. The good news for Gene and I was that we had graduated in the top ten percent of our OCS Class and would therefore be flying fixed wing trainers in the Air Force which guaranteed that we would be flying fixed wing aircraft in the Marines and not helicopters. That was important because the Marine Corps and Army were losing helicopters and their flight crews at an alarming rate in Viet Nam.

At graduation our Drill Instructor pinned our Second Lieutenant Bars on us and gave us our first salute. Out of the original sixty-six Candidates, less than fifty graduated. We were Marine Officers, and Gene and I were on our way to Selma, Alabama.

CHAPTER TWO

EARNING AIR FORCE WINGS

Gene and I arrived at Craig Air Force Base in Selma, Alabama in January of 1969. It was two years after the famous Selma Bridge March led by Rev. Martin Luther King. We joined a class of about sixty Air Force potential pilots and five other Marines. Our class also included three potential pilots from Iran. Gene and I were assigned a small apartment unit on base with two bedrooms and a central living area/kitchen.

We were all assigned our gray Nomex flame resistant flight suits and our first pilot name tags with our name and rank. We each also wore our respective service caps. Our class had students from the Air Force Academy and various ROTC units from different universities.

We started Academics immediately. We learned why and how aircraft fly. We learned about Visual Flight Rules (VFR) and Instrument Flight Rules (IFR). We learned about weather, flight patterns, and details about the first aircraft we were to attempt to fly.

The Air force Pilot Training started the pilots with the Cessna T-41 Mescalero. It was essentially a small, single engine, propeller driven, Cessna 172. To begin flying we were bussed out to a small remote airfield focused just on T-41 pilot training. The

T-41 was slow, safe and to move forward each of us would have to fly the T-41 for around thirty hours and also fly our first Solo.

I enjoyed the flying immediately. To be able to fly high above the earth and look down on the roads and houses and towns was fun. We flew with a yoke (half a steering wheel) and the throttle was a knob that was pushed in or pulled out to change engine propeller speed. We learned to always expect trouble and to anticipate the engine failing. If the engine died you would have to identify the best area to try to land which might be a grassy field or a farm road. To practice the instructor pilot would suddenly pull the engine throttle to idle and inform you that you had just lost your engine. You would begin looking for a suitable place to land with no telephone or electric wires in sight. As the aircraft came down fairly close to landing the instructor would then push the throttle up to full power and climb the aircraft back to altitude.

When it was time for a pilot to fly his first solo flight, the instructor pilot and student would do one or two takeoffs and landings, and then the Instructor would pull off to a taxi-way. He would get out of the aircraft and then lean back in.

"Do five takeoffs and landings!" he would say and then shout "Good Luck!"

He would then shut the aircraft door and walk away. We all knew who was going to be flying a solo flight each day. As each solo pilot would take off, all the rest of us on the ground would go outside to watch the show, and it was definitely a show. The solo pilot and plane would generally take off just fine and then enter the traffic pattern flying around the air field. When it was his turn to land, the pilot would line up with the runway, gradually come down and when close to the ground the show would begin. Sometimes the T-41 might go too nose high and the plane would suddenly fall on to the runway and bounce maybe ten feet into the air. At that point, we could hear the aircraft engine start to rev up just as the plane came down again, then bounce and start to climb back into the air. At each bounce the spectators would cheer and groan, look at each other, and laugh; but then we would each grow silent as we realized we might be next.

From my personal experience I can tell you that when my instructor pilot started to get out of the aircraft, I wanted to get out of the plane WITH him. However, I knew that wouldn't work, so I just swallowed and proceeded to do my first solo take-off and landing. It was exciting, and fortunately, for me, relatively uneventful. It was one of the first times I realized that when airborne I had to handle the flying and landing and any emergencies all by myself. No one else in the world could assist or save me. I was on my own. A valuable lifetime lesson.

We lost a couple of pilot candidates early during the T-41 training as they failed or did a voluntary drop out. Thankfully, we lost none to any mishaps.

The next aircraft we flew was the Cessna T-37 which was known as the Tweet. It had this nickname because when the engines were running it made an extremely loud, high pitched, annoying whistle. In the T-37, the pilot and Instructor pilot sat side by side. Each pilot had a control stick between their legs and two throttles on their left. It was a small, two engine, jet aircraft that set very low to the ground. It was our first experience in a jet. It was relatively fast, complex and serious next to the T-41.

We needed to fly approximately ninety hours in the T-37. The pilots were divided into two Flights. The two Flights would fly at different times of the day but use the same Ready Room and the same aircraft. Gene and I were in the same Flight with one other Marine, Bill. Gene and I had the same Instructor Pilot. He was a small, bald man with a sarcastic sense of humor and a reputation of being extremely demanding.

Again we were continuing with academics; learning about our aircraft, jet engines, and now learning about aerobatics and formation flying. Then it was finally time to fly a jet. We were now working from Craig Air Base so it was busy with T-37 and T-38 aircraft taking off and landing. The aircraft was very loud. The taxi was interesting, and confusing with the amount of radio communication with ground control and other aircraft and specific taxi instructions. Finally we were cleared for takeoff and rolled out onto the runway and suddenly we took off. The acceleration was just exhilarating with a jet engine! It was new to have a control stick between your legs controlled by your right hand and dual engine throttles for your left.

In the T-37, we first learned to do aileron rolls, moving the stick left or right causing the aircraft to roll around its central axis, like rolling on the floor. It was interesting to be upside down and then right side up. Next came loops, where you simply built up your airspeed and pulled the stick towards your lap while holding the wings steady. The nose of the aircraft would begin pointing straight up and your airspeed would be dying then you would be upside down over the top and then flying straight down at the ground with airspeed building until you leveled back out. It was my first time going straight up and watching my airspeed die and my first time going straight down watching my airspeed build.

Then we learned to do an Immelmann. Again you would build up your speed and pull the stick into your lap, and go vertical until you reached the altitude you wanted. Then you would roll back level only now you were thousands of feet above where you started and you were going the opposite direction. We learned to do Barrel Rolls as if you were flying your aircraft around the outside of a barrel. These were all new to me and thrilling. Initially I was not doing the flying and felt sick. I almost had to puke into my glove while doing the aerobatics. Luckily I didn't. We had one pilot who puked in his glove every single training flight before he earned his wings. He later became a fighter pilot. I really respected his persistence.

We also learned to join close to other airplanes and fly in formation. This meant you would be some distance behind another aircraft, and then have to build your speed so you could catch the other aircraft but not go screaming by them. Or you could approach so slowly you couldn't complete the join up. You learned to judge distances and airspeed just by eye. Once joined you had to fly with your cockpit five feet off the other aircraft's wing tip. This took concentration, but was essential while flying formation during the day and at night and entering clouds and if you could not stay close turning, climbing, descending, you would lose sight of your lead aircraft, which is extremely dangerous. It is extremely dangerous to have two aircraft in close proximity to each other without a visual sighting.

Even after all of this, the most serious maneuver we needed to master in order to pass in the T-37 training, was the spin recovery. This meant you had placed the aircraft into a spin, and then recover control. These were dreaded and definitely no fun. A spin meant you first flew the aircraft so slow that it actually stalled, and you were just falling like a rock. A spinning rock at that! You would then move the stick in one direction and suddenly the aircraft would spin, out of control, and you would be flopping around and falling out of the sky. You would be looking at the ground spinning and every so often you would look at the altimeter and see that you were losing thousands of feet in altitude. YIKES!

To pass the spin test you would have to learn to go through a specific recovery process until the aircraft stopped spinning and began flying again. The instructor pilots, when commenting on how long they had left in their training command tour of duty would simply say,

"Well, I have five hundred and eighty spins left."

It was the first time I was really aware of why having an ejection seat sounded like a good idea.

Again we each had to do our first solo flight in the Tweet. When the solo pilot would land after his first solo flight all the other pilot classmates would greet him and tie him up to a flag pole and spray him down with a hose.

At each level and with each aircraft, every flight was scored and logged in order to eventually determine Class Rankings, and to ensure you were ready for the next phase of training. If you failed a flight you then had to take a Seventy Seven flight with another instructor. If you failed that you would have to take an Eighty Eight flight with a senior instructor. The final flight was with the squadron Commander. It was a Ninety Nine flight and if you failed you were considered washed out and you were immediately eliminated from the program. Everyone knew when a student was taking one of these flights, and the pressure on the pilot and the tension in the Ready Room was intense.

Each step we took required academic classes and tests associated with the flying lessons and actual flight tests. Everything was competitive, and it was always understood that not everyone would make it. Eliminations were expected and occurred frequently. A few candidates just decided they didn't like the flying, the pressure, or they just couldn't get comfortable... and they would drop out.

We also had physical fitness exercises and games. We would play football, basketball, soccer, have track races, etc. We had six Iranian pilots in our class and they would love it when we played soccer. That game they knew, the other games not so much. After working out, we typically would finish by running laps around the track. The Marines, like myself, would always try to lead that exercise just to prove we were Marines. Luckily we had one Marine, Bill that was about 6' 3'' and a runner. He would effortlessly run off and leave everyone struggling behind him.

We also had Happy Hour and squadron parties that built the comradery. When I joined my first few Marine and Air Force Units it was very different to be surrounded by men from New York City, New Orleans, California, Chicago, Alabama, Salt Lake City and Iran. You were competing with everyone but you were also part of a new team made up of men very much like yourself in many ways. We made new friendships fast and we had a lot of fun.

After we had completed T-37 training, a few of us decided to drive down to Pensacola, Florida and watch the Blue Angels Flight Demonstration Team. Although most of the candidates were driving hot cars, one of my friends, Headstone, was driving a big (and old) Buick convertible. We had a great time driving down and checking into a hotel. We goofed around on the beach looking to meet women, and failed as usual. That first night we were driving from one bar on the way to another. With us was Randy, who had drunk more than anyone else. Suddenly, while sitting in the center of the back seat, Randy reached forward and moved the transmission into Park. The car immediately slid to a stop as Headstone managed to keep it on the road. We yelled at Randy and he just laughed. That night I went out of my room to get a Coke out of a dispenser and found Randy sitting on the outside stairs nude. We got him up and back into his room. Would it surprise you to learn that Randy dropped out of the program the next week?

On Saturday we drove onto the Naval Base and watched the Blue Angels do their flight demonstration show. They were flying Blue F-4 Phantoms. Those Phantoms were extremely loud and looked so mean that I started to dream that maybe one day I could be flying one of those aircraft. They did a great show and following that we jumped back in the convertible and headed back up to Selma and our next training challenge: the T-38.

During that first six months we discovered that Selma was a small town and all the women had been taken. We would therefore roam out to Montgomery, Alabama on weekends and try to get lucky. We, of course failed.

The Northrop Talon T-38 was the final aircraft we got to fly in Air force training. It was a two engine jet trainer. The Talon was always white, with a needle nose and small wings. It looked fast, and it WAS fast. It had Afterburners! It could fly faster than the speed of sound—or Mach 1. That was one of the first things you did in the T-38; fly up to an altitude of 30,000 feet, plug in the afterburners, and wait until your Mach indicator (speedometer) showed you were now going supersonic. That amounts to a little less than seven hundred miles per hour. It would not be a big deal to you in the cockpit, as you could not tell you had just gone supersonic unless you were looking at your Mach indicator gauge. It would just hop a little. Of course, on the ground a sonic boom was very loud so you could only fly supersonic in certain areas that did not have civilians below.

In the Talon the pilot always sat in front and the instructor would sit in the rear. The instructor pilot would also have a stick and throttles so he could maneuver and recover the aircraft if the student screwed up. Once again we learned how to do take offs and landings, how to fly aerobatics, and how to join up with other aircraft and fly formations. The aerobatics were more fun in the Talon as occasionally you used afterburner, and the loops and Immelmann were much larger. This was very important training as they were the building blocks to be able to fly Air Combat Maneuvering.

We also spent time learning how to fly Instrument Flight Rules, or IFR. We flew in a T-38 simulator. We learned that when flying in clouds you could not trust your natural senses. If you started a slow roll or turn, soon it would feel like you were flying level, while you were actually turning and maybe beginning to dive at the earth. In the T-38 you would pull a canvas shield that would make it so you could not see outside the aircraft. You had to focus intently on your instruments and trust them. We learned how to navigate both visually and using instruments. How to fly from one point to another without being able to see the ground. How to read an approach plate and follow the instructions so that you could land your plane in sequence with many others while not seeing anybody. It was very odd to fly in clouds, pull out the correct approach plate and secure it on your knee pad, read and follow the instructions about the direction to turn, altitude to fly, and airspeed to maintain all while keeping the aircraft level and under control. It would be such a relief when flying an approach in weather conditions when you suddenly got low enough to break out of the clouds and be able to see the ground and the runway, hopefully, right in front of you.

Near the end of flight training we had two special flights. The first was when I got to fly my first cross country. That required you to select a Navy, Air Force or Marine base where a T-37 could land and refuel and the crews could spend a night at a strange base. We selected Patrick Air Force Base in Cocoa Beach, Florida. The flight was uneventful and it was fun to land at a strange base and park the aircraft in a new transient aircraft line. We checked into the Bachelor Officers Quarter (BOQ) and then headed out to Cocoa Beach to eat. Lucky for us that night NASA was doing a rocket launch. They were to launch and recover a monkey. I remember sitting out on the sand drinking Black Russians and lamenting the potential fate of the monkey. That monkey ended up helping change the name of Patrick Air Force Base to Patrick Space Force Base, as it is called today!

The second special flight was my first solo night cross country. It was during this trip when for the first time (and unfortunately not the last time) I did something stupid during the flight. Stupid to the point where I thought "Wow, you could have killed yourself, Greg."

The idea of this flight was to have the young pilot fly a solo night mission in the T-38. Rather than staying in the comfortable area around Craig Air Force Base, however, the pilot would instead fly over to Montgomery, Alabama, navigate over Atlanta, Georgia and then proceed to Gulfport, Mississippi before finally returning back to Craig AFB.

The takeoff was uneventful as was the climbing up and leveling off at 35,000 feet. It was a little hazy but beautiful and quiet. After a bit of flying a thought came to me. Why not do an aileron roll? Of course, one reason not to do a night aileron roll was that we had been taught that doing a night aileron roll was very dangerous.

The Talon had a very impressive roll rate. You could move the stick a couple of inches to either side of the center position and the aircraft would roll seven hundred and twenty degrees in one second. That was two complete rolls in a second.

But I was young and cocky and I thought... Why not! I initiated the roll and immediately became disoriented. Had I rolled a half roll? A full roll? A roll and a half? Looking outside the canopy I discovered I could not distinguish between the lights on the ground and the stars in the sky. They looked exactly alike. The immediate question became should I keep rolling?

I looked at the altimeter that shows how high above the ground you are. The needle was spinning and I was losing altitude fast. I looked at another gauge and it showed I was diving. If I'm diving but upside down if I pull the nose I will be going straight down. I start to panic a little! My mind began to race. I began thinking I may have to eject and then if I survive I will be out of the flight program and back to the Marines and Viet Nam as a grunt.

I took a deep breath and studied the instruments again and began to figure out what I needed to do to level the aircraft. I stopped my roll and my dive. At that time I received a call from Atlanta Air Traffic Control asking if I am OK. I now realized that I had lost TEN THOUSAND feet of altitude. I was at an extremely dangerous altitude where other aircraft going in opposite directions would not expect me. I immediately turned off my IFF (Identification Friend or Foe). That is a box that puts out data so that the air traffic controllers and other aircraft could know my position and my altitude.

I immediately started to climb and turned to make sure I was still heading towards Atlanta. I quickly arrived at thirty five thousand feet only to realize the aircraft felt very sluggish. I glanced at my airspeed indicator and to my horror realized I was extremely slow and very close to stalling. Sheesh! If the Talon stalls and goes into a spin I am done for. The T-38 is so difficult to recover it is something we never even wasted time practicing. On top of that I was by myself and it was dark outside.

Meanwhile Atlanta Air Traffic Control again asked me if I was OK. I replied that I was. I immediately turned the IFF back on and lit the afterburners. That quickly got me back to speed but I realized I was now a big flare in the sky with the afterburner lit. Any other student or airline pilot in the area could now clearly see my afterburner flame. I got to the right airspeed and course direction. I settled down and continued my flight, uneventfully landing back at Craig.

I slipped into the squadron Ready Room after chocking my aircraft. I am awaited a call from my instructor or the squadron Commander wondering what the hell was I doing out there.

Time passed and nothing happened. I snuck off to my car and drive home. Wondering if I slipped through the potential noose. I guess I did. Did I mention I've always been lucky?

LESSON LEARNED: If they tell you don't do something because it is dangerous what they probably are telling you is that someone has died trying to do it so DON'T DO IT!

After six months we were allowed to move off the base, and so a group of us moved into an apartment complex. Gene had gotten married to his sweetheart Sue, and moved into one of the apartments. I moved into the same apartment complex with Johnnie from Tennessee and BJ from South Carolina. We became close friends. Everybody was driving hot cars and mine was a brand new 1969 Red Ford Mustang Mach One. Johnnie had a black GTO and others had Corvettes. Life was good. We could see the light at the end of the tunnel.

During the day we would fly, attend classes, and study. On the weekends we would fool around in the pool. At night we would crowd into one room to watch shows on the first color TV we had ever seen. We watched the Johnny Cash and Glen Campbell shows. One night we all crammed into one room to watch the Moon Landing. That was exciting.

Near the end of my year with the Air Force, I was phoning and writing Susan, a beautiful young woman whom I had met at Washington State University. I flew out to Seattle in July and over a weekend I proposed.

She said "Yes!"

She and her family did all the wedding planning. I just flew out to Seattle in early October for a long weekend, and that's when we were married. Then, with no honeymoon, she flew back with me to Selma, Alabama where the next morning at 4:30 AM I was back flying at the squadron. We eventually moved into a tiny rental duplex where when moving from the living room to the kitchen one had to walk through the bedroom. It was hot and humid so we bought a huge airplane fan so we could sleep. We only had one car so Susan would often be left at home with no transportation. But we were young and in love so it was OK.

I have to admit I was smitten when I saw my first McDonnell Douglas F4 Phantom Fighter jet up close. Gene and I were walking along the Craig flight line and there parked in front of the Base Operations sat two McDonnell Douglas Marine Corps F-4 Phantoms. They looked huge and dirty grey. The jet intakes were enormous as were the tires. We went around to the rear and looked at the huge afterburner nozzles and tried to imagine what that must feel like when those afterburners were lit. It was dripping hydraulic fluid and still had its drag chute deployed and laying on the ground behind the aircraft. The drag chute was a big parachute that would be deployed when landing to slow down the aircraft before applying the brakes. We looked at the arresting tail hook which was to stop the aircraft when it landed on an aircraft carrier. We commented that although it was big, it looked too small to stop this monster.

The Phantom was a hulking, mean, serious looking war plane with its stabilator in the rear swooping down towards the ground and the end of each wing lifting at an angle towards the sky. The nose was huge where it hid the radar but it also appeared to hunker down towards the ground. It had a single large belly fuel tank that could be jettisoned if needed.

At first inspection I had an immediate crush, but that was just the start. The Marine aircrew came out and repacked the drag chute themselves. As we watched I think they noticed our Marine covers (caps) which were unusual on an Air Force Base. The Phantom started its two engines and it was so loud you couldn't talk to someone standing right next to you. The Phantom pilot and plane captain went through their ground checks and then the Phantoms began to taxi. As he passed us, the lead pilot turned his head and saluted us. Ok, now I was seriously impressed.

When the Phantoms reached the end of the runway they did their engine run ups where the brakes are set and the engines are put up to 100% and all the engine gauges are checked before takeoff begins. The tremendously loud sound echoed around the base off of every hanger and building. I noticed that all the activity on the airfield had stopped as everyone on base was watching. These were not the common little T-37s or sleek T-38s. The Phantoms rolled out onto the runway. They began to roll for takeoff and the thunder of their engines reached us. We then heard the afterburners light. It was just at dusk so you could not only hear the roar when the afterburners engaged, but you could see the flame shoot out the back of both engines maybe twenty feet on both aircraft. The noise was so different than anything the T-37 or T-38 aircraft made when taking off. It was just awesome! The Phantoms left the ground and their landing gear was raised with both aircraft in tight formation. The aircraft stayed low to the deck, quickly picking up speed. Both aircraft smoothly picked up their noses till they were going sixty degrees up, came out of burner, and went into a light cloud level.

Any male pilot that had experienced that and didn't have a woody should have dropped out of the program. My best friend and fellow Marine Gene and I just looked at each other. If we made it through Air Force Flight School there was a good chance we could be assigned to that aircraft. We could be flying the Marine Corps F4 Phantom II. I was now officially in love.

In January we had our Graduation ceremony. Bill made it exciting by showing up at the ceremony wearing his Dress Blue Uniform. The only problem was, that he was supposed to be wearing his Class A Green Uniform. He immediately rushed back to his car and made a high speed trip to his apartment and changed his uniform. Then he made another high speed trip back arriving just in time as the ceremony began.

The ceremony was formal but short. We received our Air Force Wings. Susan pinned mine on me. Out of the sixty five students that had started the program a little over forty graduated. In the Air Force you had the opportunity to request the type of aircraft you desired to fly and if your class ranking was high enough you might get it. The number one man in the class chose fighters. Some chose larger transport aircraft perhaps thinking of the potential for airline careers in the future. Those that finished lower in the class just got what they were assigned.

It was difficult to say goodbye to both our instructors and our classmates. Because we were heading back to the Marines, it would be unusual to see our Air Force comrades again. We had an unusually close class and I can tell you that thirty years after our graduation, everyone showed up for our class reunion. Since then we have had three more.

At that time all we knew was that Gene and I had hopes to be flying the F-4 Phantom. Before doing that we would have to earn our Navy Wings. That would begin in January 1970.

CHAPTER THREE

EARNING NAVY WINGS

Graduation from Air Force Flight Class 70-05 was over. Gene and I had finished in the top half of our class and were going to join the Marine Corps pilots.

We packed up our few things in a U-Haul truck and drove to Cherry Point Marine Corps Air Base in Havelock, North Carolina. There we joined VMFAT-201, a USMC training squadron. Susan and I rented a small trailer to live in and bought a small sports car so that each of us would have a car. I got the little TR-4 which was great except if you went over fifty five miles per hour the roof would come off, and you could see the ground through a couple of holes in the floor too.

We learned that in a Marine squadron you had a Commanding Officer (The Skipper), The Executive Officer (XO- Discipline), S-3 Operations Officer (OPSO- Flight Operations), Aviation Maintenance Officer (AMO- Keep the planes flying), S-4 (Logistics), S-2 (Intelligence), Safety (Fly safe) and NATOPS (Fly by the Book). Every Marine and Navy Ready Room has four designated chairs in the front row for the CO, XO, OPSO and AMO.

We got our green flight suits, our steel toed flight boots, a G-suit, a safety harness and flight helmets. Again we started taking Academics to learn the aircraft. Sometimes the classes were taught by pilots returning from Viet Nam. That added a different flavor to what we were learning.

We soon realized that in the same way we were somewhat outsiders as Marines in an Air Force Training squadron, we were now viewed again as outsiders. We were pilots with Silver Air Force Wings joining a squadron of young Marine pilots with Gold Navy Wings. They had gone through Naval Flight Training. They had landed on an aircraft carrier. We knew we would be tested and have to prove ourselves once again. Three of us checked into the squadron and within four weeks one of our group had been washed out. Gene and I hung in.

Once again we started with Academics learning about the F-4. We studied its electronics, hydraulics, fuel systems, engines, instruments, and missiles. We studied the cockpit and it was very complex with gauges and switches and circuit breakers. We learned about the Ejection Seats and the Drag Chutes. For the first time we would be flying an aircraft with a Radar System and we began to learn how to fly radar intercepts. We flew in simulators.

We also had some ground exercises that were very interesting. One included going into a pressure chamber where they could gradually simulate different altitudes. One of the tests was to go up to over twenty five thousand feet altitude and remove your oxygen mask and begin to learn what your individual symptoms of hypoxia were. You would be given a three year olds puzzle to try to put various shapes in the right place. Soon I was slurring my words and trying to put a triangle piece into a square space and I was giggling at my failure. If left without oxygen I would have soon passed out. The idea was to learn what my hypoxia symptoms were so I could recognize if I was beginning to have an oxygen system problem when flying.

We also were put into a mock ejection seat and the big device simulated a crash landing into the water upside down. You would be strapped into your ejection seat and the device would crash into the water and go inverted. You would then have to release your restraints, escape the cockpit while upside down and then swim to the surface. We also were pulled behind a jeep while strapped in a parachute. We were launched into the air a couple of hundred feet high and then the chute would be released so we could learn how to successfully land if we had to eject and land in a parachute.

We started our Navy training in the Douglas TA-4 Sky Hawk aircraft. The A-4 was an Attack aircraft which meant in combat it would be used primarily to provide ground attack by dropping bombs. It was a sturdy, sub-sonic aircraft. Larger than the T-38 but smaller than the F-4. Next we had to learn Naval Aviation terms and procedures. We had to learn the TA-4 cockpit and systems backwards and forwards. We learned how to take off and land the Skyhawk. The Skyhawk would also land on aircraft carriers, so it had a tail hook. That led to a whole new way of landing that we had to learn.

In the Air Force the air bases featured long runways and so when landing the goal was to make the landing smooth. In the Navy smooth landings were not desired. When landing the objective was to fly a specific airspeed and Angle of Attack (AOA) so that you touched down at a specific point on a carrier. At that point your tail hook would engage one of four arresting cables and stop the aircraft suddenly. If you were too fast or your nose was too high or too flat you would not engage the cable and all sorts of bad things could happen. There was a special lighting system within the cockpit to help you accomplish this feat. When you were at the right Angle Of Attack the lights would be green. If you were too steep or too shallow it would turn red and an aural warning sound would start soft at first and then louder. You would also look out near the end of the runway and there would be another set of lights. If you kept three lights in a parallel line you were on track. However, if the middle light starting going high then you were going to land long and if the middle light started to go below the two side lights then you were going to land short. If you kept the lights aligned until touch down you would engage the arresting cable. Also at the end of the runway there would be a Landing Signal Operator (LSO) and he would be talking to you to help you maintain the correct Angle Of Attack, the correct airspeed and the correct line up with the runway. Sheesh!

So Navy landings were not smooth. They were rather hard and abrupt, but they were precise. We practiced landing until we were ready to land with the tail hook down and catch an arresting cable. That meant you would fly down to touchdown at an airspeed of about one hundred and thirty six knots (157 mph), the hook would grab the cable and within a second or two you would be stopped. If your eyeballs didn't fly out of your head and hit the canopy it was actually fun.

We also had the opportunity to do a catapult launch on the ground. That is where you would taxi to a specific spot and they would attach a catapult sled to the bottom of your aircraft. You would put the throttles up to one hundred percent (Military power), the pilot would salute the aircraft plane captain. He would return the salute and suddenly you would be pressed into the back of your ejection seat as your aircraft accelerated to takeoff speed (over 150 knots) in just a couple of seconds. You would then rotate the nose upward and you found yourself flying. Exhilarating is a word that does not do that experience justice!

We also learned to drop bombs. On most Attack and Fighter/ Attack aircraft the bombs are attached to pylons that hang from the wings. A typical practice bomb was about three feet long and maybe weighed twenty-five pounds. In the nose of the bomb was a small shotgun shell that would produce a tiny amount of smoke when it hit the ground so you could see how accurate your bombing had been.

To start bombing you would fly to a bombing range and acquire the target. You would then circle your aircraft above the target until cleared to attack. Bombing runs were typically in a ten, thirty or forty five degree dive. The type of dive you used depended on the type of target, the ordnance you carried and the enemy defenses. For example, if you were dropping napalm, you would be at ten degrees or level and at four hundred knots. At that altitude and airspeed you were a target for enemy small arms but your accuracy was likely very good. The common dive angle was thirty degrees and around four hundred and fifty knots. That felt steep but controllable. You could release five hundred pound bombs with good accuracy. The expectation was that enemy ground forces would fire anti-aircraft guns, and small heat seeking missiles at you. The forty five degree dive felt very steep and you would drop the bombs at around five hundred knots. This would be used where the enemy anti-aircraft forces were formidable.

On a thirty degree bombing run you would circle the target and then roll in. You have a small reticle with a lighted aiming circle. You level your wings at thirty degrees nose down. Your airspeed begins to build. If there is a wind you have to account for it. If you don't account for the wind then a tail wind will send the bomb long and a head wind will drop it short where side winds will have predictable effects. If you are too slow the bomb will land short. If you are too fast the bomb will go long. So the goal is to have the reticle approaching the target, making adjustments for the wind, at an exact thirty degree dive angle and exactly four hundred and fifty knots. You then hit the pickle button on your stick just as the reticle highlights the target. Immediately after release, you begin a four G pull out or you will impact the ground just beyond the target. It was a lot to learn, but it was also fun, and I discovered I was pretty good at bombing. You also learned that during the dive and after the release it was smart to "jink the aircraft." Jinking is intentionally changing your direction suddenly, to throw off the previous smooth tracking solution of the anti-aircraft guns. Of course, after release you were jinxing also because you were closer to the ground and they might be firing shoulder mounted missiles at you. A 4G jink towards the missile is intended to cause a miss from shoulder mounted or air-to-air fired missiles.

Finally we had to learn Air Combat Maneuvering or ACM. If you encounter enemy aircraft in time of war and engage in a fight… that is ACM. So every Fighter Pilot must learn to fly ACM and eventually how well you flew ACM would determine how you are regarded in the squadron. The TA-4 was a relatively easy aircraft to fly ACM. It turned really well, it had good fuel preservation, the visibility out of the cockpit was good and the aircraft didn't have special tricks you needed to know if you got slow. It was not supersonic but that was OK. It did not a have great thrust to weight ratio so building airspeed and fighting vertical was a challenge, but that was offset because it turned so well and so it was good in a horizontal fight.

When flying ACM you typically see the other aircraft and try to maneuver behind it. Once behind it you can fire heat seeking missiles or fire your Gatling gun. However, to do that it is hard work. You are pulling four to six G's which means if you weigh two hundred pounds on the ground you now weigh over one thousand pounds.

Moving your head to keep watching the other aircraft becomes difficult. Your oxygen system starts forcing oxygen into your lungs so talking becomes more difficult. You are wearing a G suit that goes from your waist down to your ankles. It starts to fill with air and builds pressure in the lower part of your body so that the blood doesn't go down into your feet and out of your head (your eyeballs loose blood first then you pass out) due to the G's you are pulling. Occasionally you have to push the stick forward and suddenly you are pushing negative G's and your head is hitting the canopy and all the dust and crap that may be in the cockpit is floating up around your head. At the same time you are focusing on maneuvering against the aircraft you are fighting but if you are experienced you are also looking around to make sure your adversary's wingman is not closing in to shoot you down.

ACM is totally demanding. Your heart is pounding, your alertness is at its highest point. Your adrenaline is spiking. You are coordinating your hands on the stick and the throttles. Your feet are using the rudders. Your eyes are tracking the adversary, your altitude, your airspeed, your missile range, your G's, the sun, your fuel state. You are talking to your wingman and in an F-4 your RIO (Radar Intercept Officer). It is exhausting and awesome.

When we finally completed ACM in the TA-4, we had progressed to the point where we were awarded our gold Naval Aviator Wings. Both Gene and I had done well. We could choose our aircraft. Surprise, we chose the Phantom!

The McDonnell Douglas F-4 Phantom is big. It is fifty eight feet long and thirty eight feet wide. When filled with JP-4 fuel it weighs over thirty six thousand pounds. It can carry over eighteen thousand pounds of weapons, three fuel tanks, four AIM-7 Raytheon Sparrow Radar Missiles, multiple Raytheon AIM-9 Sidewinder Heat Seeking missiles and thousands of pounds of bombs and rockets. It has two huge jet engines that in full afterburner can generate over thirty six thousand pounds of thrust. It has a large arresting hook. It carries a pilot who sits in front and a Radar Intercept Officer (RIO) that sits behind the pilot. The Phantom has a powerful pulse-Doppler radar system that could find other aircraft out over thirty miles away. It has two Martin Baker ejections seats. On the right side is a refueling probe that can be extended in order to take on fuel when airborne.

When you are sitting in the Phantom you are close to ten feet above the ground. On your left you have two throttles. Between your legs you have a control stick with which you fly the aircraft, fire missiles, drop bombs, lock the radar on a target or trim the aircraft so it flies steady. You have a small handle to raise your flaps, a small hook to lower your arresting hook. You also have a button to extend the refueling probe. In front of you sits maybe twenty gauges. On both sides are more circuit breakers than you can count. This is all to say the cockpit of the F-4 is impressive, and before flying it, YOU will require weeks of academics and simulator time.

I clearly remember the first time I flew the Phantom. I remember approaching the Phantom and doing the preflight routine for real. I then started the engines and went through the preflight routine with the Plane Captain. Finally saluting the Plane Captain we began to taxi. Sitting up so high and feeling the powerful engines, I felt like a king. We taxied out to the end of the runway and did our run-up checks at military power (100%). We then taxied out to the end of the runway and my RIO requested take off clearance. Once clearance was received I released the brakes and for the first time moved the throttles forward up into full afterburner. BAM! The aircraft literally felt like it jumped forward! I had never felt such acceleration, and with the nose starting to feel light I saw immediately that we were passing through takeoff speed. I pulled back on the stick and we left the ground quickly. I raised the landing gear and flaps and we were accelerating through two hundred twenty knots. Soon we were climbing out at three hundred and fifty knots.

On this first F-4 flight we just did the basics. We climbed up into a Military Training Area over the Atlantic Ocean. We accelerated to four hundred and fifty knots and I was instructed to bank the aircraft and pull six G's. At six G's your G-Suit is fully filled with air and it is pressing your legs and abdomen keeping the blood in the upper half of your body. Remember, at those G's if you weigh two hundred pounds you now weigh twelve hundred pounds. It is difficult to turn your head, move your arms, and because your oxygen system begins pressing oxygen into your face mask, it becomes difficult to talk. I remember thinking that when we begin flying ACM, we will encounter these conditions constantly. It is most definitely hard work.

We then climbed the Phantom to over forty five thousand feet in altitude. Then we lowered the nose and went into full afterburner, soon reaching supersonic speed and accelerating to about Mach 1.6 (or well over one thousand miles per hour). Flying straight up and straight down I began to appreciate the F4's power and stability.

At the end of the flight we did some slow speed flying. In the F-4 that meant you slowed down to under two hundred knots, holding the nose up until you were almost vertical and it felt like you are standing on your tail. As you flew more and more vertical, your airspeed kept getting slower and slower. The nose started feeling very heavy and sluggish. That was the danger zone for the F-4. At that slow airspeed (right above stall speed) when you tried to maneuver the aircraft by moving the stick left or right, the aircraft would go the opposite direction. You would begin to enter the zone where the aircraft might go into a spin.

The F-4 in a spin required a certain set of steps to recover, including pushing the stick forward until you were heading straight at the ground in order to build up airspeed. When you once again have sufficient speed (Speed is Life!), you pull out of the nose down dive. That recovery in the F-4 took about 10,000 feet of altitude. What I learned was that when flying the F-4 at slow speeds was that you had to stop using the stick to turn, and instead used your feet by moving the rudder petals. So imagine fighting another aircraft and going straight up and down (and maybe even upside down) when you suddenly find yourself super slow and have to quickly transition to using the rudders while holding the stick centered. It was one of the areas where really experienced F-4 pilots or just superior pilots gained advantages over other F-4 pilots. Also, it was critical to understand that if you lost control of the Phantom at below ten thousand feet, you would most likely have to eject. By the way, that is one reason why America, introduced Rules Of Engagement which included not engaging in a slow speed fight under ten thousand feet of altitude. You knocked off the fight when reaching ten thousand feet if in a slow speed fight (knock it off meant stop fighting).

After four months of learning to fly the F-4 we completed our training. That week the Operations Officer from VMFA-451, one of the Marine F-4 Gun Squadrons, visited and recruited both Gene and I to join the Warlords. We were going to be Phantom pilots!

CHAPTER FOUR

THE WARLORDS

Once again the four of us packed up a U-Haul truck and we moved down to Beaufort, South Carolina, home of the Beaufort Marine Corps Air Station and the VMFA-451 Warlords.

Beaufort, South Carolina is a small town located on the Broad River and surrounded by marshlands. Beaufort has been featured in several movies representing old southern homes with large porches, surrounded by huge trees and overlooking a lazy river. These movies include *"The Great Santini,"* and *"The Big Chill."* A fellow Marine took Susan and I out to this Island that was being developed and I remember thinking why would anyone invest in this. I thought all it had was mosquitoes. Well that Island is now known as Hilton Head. I didn't buy...another brilliant real estate move on my part.

The Marine Corps Air Base had two long crossing runways. When we first got to the base it featured three F-4J squadrons, an A-6 Intruder squadron and an A-4 Sky Hawk squadron. All the squadrons reported to Marine Air Group-31 (MAG-31). MAG-31 reported to the Second Marine Air Wing (2ND MAW) located up at Cherry Point, North Carolina.

Gene and I reported to VMFA-451, the Warlords. A typical Gun squadron would have fifteen to eighteen aircraft and a compliment of two hundred to three hundred Marines including about twenty pilots and twenty RIOS. Gene and I were the youngest and newest pilots in the squadron.

Since I had not been to any secondary occupation schools, my first squadron secondary job became to take on Marines that were failing the Physical Fitness Training (PFT) and improve their performance. By the way, the Marine Corps takes the PFT seriously. The PFT test consisted of only three things: Pull-ups, sit-ups and a three mile run. First you would have to hang from the bar and then pull your chin over the bar at least four times. Twenty would max out the pull-ups. Sit-ups would require you to do the most you could do in two minutes. Eighty would max out the sit-ups. Then would come the three mile run. Eighteen minutes would Max Out the three mile run. Depending on your age, you could pass the three mile run if you just kept running the entire distance at a reasonable pace. However, if you started to walk it became almost impossible. So each day I would have two to five Marines meet up with me and we would do the pull-ups, sit-ups and then go for a three mile run. During the summer it was hot and humid in Beaufort. Modern running shoes had not yet been introduced to the United States. Imagine the fun I had as a young Second Lieutenant with no real Marine experience running with a couple of Marines twice my age, who had been in the corps forever. That was fun.

When in VMFA-451 I learned the value of good aircraft Supply and Maintenance. We had neither in the Warlords, so the aircraft were seldom in the "UP" status, suitable to fly. Even if they were "UP" they might not have working radars. What that meant as a pilot was that you only flew maybe every other day or less. A typical flight radar intercept flight might be 1.3 hours, so a pilot might only get ten to fifteen hours of flying in a month. Since a typical ACM flight might only take .8 hours but burn all the fuel that a radar Intercept sortie took in 1.3 hours we seldom flew ACM. Squadron Flight Hours were one important measure of a squadron's success so the squadron Commander needed flight hours to compete with the other squadrons, so we seldom flew ACM.

A radar intercept mission would have you fly out to a Restricted Warning area over the water. There the two aircraft would fly opposite directions until about thirty miles separated the aircraft. The fight would then be initiated, and the RIOs with their heads bent down over their radar scopes would attempt to find the adversary aircraft. If the adversary was found, then the RIO would direct the pilot to begin a turn thirty degrees away from the adversary while the distance between the two aircraft shrunk. At some point with about ten miles separation the RIO would begin to instruct the pilot to turn to put the nose on the adversary and then at some point would then cry out to the pilot "you've got the DOT". This meant the pilot would now use his radar screen to center a Dot (the bogey) on his radar until in range for a simulated AIM -7 Sparrow missile shot. Hopefully the Pilot would have a visual sighting of the adversary aircraft by then. At that point the pilot would call "Fox 1!" If possible he would keep turning until he was behind the adversary aircraft and in Aim-9 heat seeking Sidewinder Range. When that would happen the Sidewinder would make a very distinctive metallic, growling sound and the pilot would call "Fox 2"! I can tell you being behind an adversary aircraft and hearing that very distinctive Sidewinder growl, knowing the adversary is "pretend dead," is a great feeling.

One big problem with the older Phantoms was that if you were in military power, the aircraft engines would be putting out a smoke trail. This trail was easy to see for twenty miles and would allow adversary aircraft to maneuver. The only way to avoid that smoke was to engage afterburner. That would immediately eliminate the smoke and gain you airspeed but now your fuel was being burned quickly. How quickly? A clean F-4 with no fuel tanks in full afterburner could run the Phantom out of fuel in twelve minutes. You always needed fuel to Bug Out (leave) a fight and get to home base. Therefore, before a mission the flight would agree on a Bingo Fuel state. Bingo Fuel meant you had just enough fuel to get back to home base with a little extra. Emergency Fuel meant you needed expeditious handling by Air Traffic Control or you might run out of fuel and have to eject. What this meant to the F-4 was that you were ALWAYS aware of your fuel state. If you went to afterburner to eliminate smoke then you went to minimum afterburner. If you were in an ACM fight you were always going in and out of afterburner so that you were keeping your speed up but not wasting fuel. A call of "approaching Bingo" meant start thinking about how to end the engagement and Bug Out successfully. Bingo fuel ended any fight unless you were in a real enemy ACM engagement. Then if you tried to immediately Bug Out you might be shot down trying to leave, so fuel state was always important in the F-4. Newer Phantoms eventually eliminated the smoking problems at the military throttle setting and that really helped improve the F-4 fuel consumption issue and the competitive positioning.

Because the Warlords were not flying very much we took our competitive spirit into other games. We played Acey-Deucy (a dice game like cribbage). We played ping pong. Gene and I played on the squadron basketball team with Woody and Watchdog. Our Operations Officer was a good athlete and our player coach. We ended up winning the base championship. Our Commanding Officer and the Operations Officer did not like each other too much and were very competitive. As a result the Skipper, who could not play basketball, installed a ping pong table in the Ready Room because he was very good at ping pong. Because we had the time, we ran three miles almost every day and we were in great physical condition.

A major event happened after we had been at Beaufort a couple of months. The AV-8 Harrier came to Beaufort. The Harrier was a British designed aircraft that could take off and land vertically without using the runway. It was small but was intended to provide close air support by dropping bombs and being able to fly out of advanced Marine Airfields without needing established runways. I remember going outside and seeing the first Harrier come over the Beaufort Airfield and then just lower itself onto the taxiway. It did not seem natural. I had no desire to fly the Harrier.

While in Beaufort I had my first few encounters with aircraft accidents, deaths and the accompanying funerals. One time an ejection seat maintenance Marine was working on the ejection seat on an aircraft in a sister squadron and something went wrong and a metal rod was ejected up into his head. He was killed instantly.

The one I remember most clearly involved a Major and a very senior pilot; call sign Tricks. He was an experienced Viet Nam veteran pilot, and the lead ACM instructor pilot in our Marine Advanced Tactical Warfare Training (MAWTS) squadron. These pilots and RIOs would come down and fly with or against the squadron pilots and RIOs and instruct them both on the ground and in the air on how to improve their ACM skills. They had to be exceptional aircrew and have many hours in the aircraft to reach the MAWTS level.

One day I was conducting a preflight on my Phantom when we were told all flights had been cancelled for the day. I wandered into the Ready Room and then learned that Tricks and his RIO, while flying a training ACM flight, had been lost. No chutes were deployed and neither was ever seen again. What was known was that the outer edge of their wing, the section that angles up, had broken off the aircraft and the Phantom had gone into a violent spin that continued into the water. Immediately all Marine and Navy Phantoms were grounded while all wings, aircraft log books, and "G-Logs" were inspected closely. G-Logs were handwritten records of what onboard G meters showed to be max-G readings for each aircraft flight.

Two days later we all attended the military funeral. It was a very somber event, with all Marines standing at attention, TAPS being played by a single bugle, a four ship of Phantoms flying a Missing Man Formation over the ceremony, and finally the widow receiving a very carefully folded American Flag. Not a dry eye in the house.

A week later the Phantoms were cleared to fly again. I was scheduled to fly ACM. You can imagine how I felt as I looked at my aircraft and scrutinized the wing joint very carefully. Then I climbed into the cockpit, was strapped in and I put on my helmet. We went through the preflight routine, I saluted the plane captain, and we began to taxi. I just kept thinking to myself that Tricks was one of the best. He had tons of hours in the F-4. He knew what he was doing and his aircraft came apart. He is dead and now I am going to go fly ACM in the same Warning Area where he went down! Of course, if you fly military aircraft you know there are going to be fatalities but you always assume it won't happen to you. So I took off and flew the mission.

I will now tell you something you need to know about fighter pilots. If you are a fighter pilot, your goal is to someday be in a fight with an enemy aircraft and its pilot, knowing that whoever loses likely dies. You can't do that if you are not very confident/cocky and pretty optimistic, and believe to a certain extent that you are invulnerable. As you become more experienced, you learn that you are NOT invulnerable. It is at this point where you begin to believe/hope that maybe you have gained enough experience and hours fighting in the aircraft that your skills and cunning will carry the day.

While in Beaufort I became close friends with Woody and Watchdog. We attended Woody's wedding where we all wore our Dress Blues with swords. When Woody and his bride departed the church they glided through our swords raised to form an archway. Truly Beautiful!

We often partied with those guys and their wives and girlfriends. That was a fun time because nobody had any money. If you were invited over for a party it was understood that you were to bring your own booze and the host and hostess would likely provide chips and dips and you would sit on the floor or on lawn furniture set up in the living room.

Soon I was sent to Marine Corps Legal School. The school was located up in Newport, Rhode Island. I drove my 1967 Austin Healey 3000 up to Newport and rented a room in a house for a few weeks. At the school I learned about the military justice system and how to conduct summary courts-martial, special courts-martial and general courts-martial. A summary court-martial was generally for minor incidents and could be conducted by me. Special courts-martial were conducted by the Commanding Officer, and General Courts-martial were held by Generals with military attorneys representing the accused. I enjoyed the school and seeing the Newport area.

When Thanksgiving came I knew I had to fly back to Beaufort and spend Thanksgiving with Susan. It was pouring down rain as I was driving the car from Newport into Boston's Logan Airport. I went through one deep puddle and because the Healey was so low to the ground, the engine suddenly failed. I had to pull over onto a side street and park the car. I was desperate because I was going to miss my flight. It was then that a big car pulled over and the driver asked if I needed help. I asked him if he could drop me off at Logan and he said that he could. I grabbed my bag and jumped in his car and we raced off to the airport where I caught my flight.

While airborne my mind was wandering and I started thinking, "Where are my car keys?" I then realized I had left my car keys in my bright red convertible sports car, in the ignition, with the doors unlocked! Boston, at the time, had the highest stolen car rate in the United States. For three days I tried to enjoy Thanksgiving while dreading what I would discover back in Boston. I ended up flying back to Boston and then had the distinct pleasure of trying to explain to a Boston Cabbie why he needed to drive around a general area and look for my car. After all, I was not certain where I had left it. Imagine my immense relief when we turned a corner and my little red sports car was sitting right where I had left it... with the keys still in the ignition! I could only explain it by thinking perhaps the Boston car thieves thought, "This must be a sting set up", and therefore just left it alone. Have I mentioned that I have always been lucky?

Now I was a pilot and the squadron Legal Officer. I had also been promoted to be First Lieutenant. I began to understand that if you were in a squadron, you were expected to go to the Officers' Club (The O Club) on Friday night for Happy Hour. You were expected to drink and learn to play dice games. You learned that aviators had reputations both for their flying skill and for their drinking escapades. Many of the aircrew in the squadron were Viet Nam Veterans. Some of them were still learning to become civilized again after a year or two in Nam—Learning that it was not OK to bite a woman on the ass at a party. It was maybe not OK to streak the bar. You learned squadron songs that were beyond rowdy and crude but were to be sung with great gusto and laughter. It was an interesting division in every squadron because the squadron had half the pilots and RIO's with combat experience, and half the squadron just learning how to be Marines and fly aircraft. I also learned that aviators generally spent between one and four years in a particular squadron. At all times you had Marines transferring to Westpac to Viet Nam or attending one of several military schools or moving to the Group or Wing level. The population of the squadron was always changing and that also meant the Skipper and XO and AMO could also be changing which meant the leadership and direction and focus of the squadron could evolve and move higher or lower.

Several times in a squadron year the Operations Officer would set up a squadron deployment. The deployment might just be for two or four aircraft to perform in an exercise or airshow, or it could be for the entire squadron to deploy. My first squadron deployment was to fly down to Roosevelt Rhodes Air Base in Puerto Rico. We deployed about ten aircraft and for two weeks we flew bombing missions, air intercept missions, and some ACM. The flying was great and I advanced to become a flight lead. For the first time I began to be called by my new call sign - SHADOW. We flew against Navy aircraft and participated in Naval Exercises. In the evenings we went to the O' Club and had a ball interacting with Navy aircrew at the Club.

If the crews got rowdy enough we might entertain the notion of Carrier Landings. This would involve the lining up of two six foot long tables set end to end. Two aircrew would then hold a towel stretched over the front end of the table while another aircrew would run and jump headfirst onto the table attempting to catch his toes on the towel and be stopped like a carrier arrested landing. Of course the table would have to be wet with beer. If that appeared too easy then the first table would begin to be rocked so that it was to resemble a rocking carrier deck.

Those times when you are flying missions during the day and partying at night forms a camaraderie that is very difficult to duplicate. Gradually, I began flying more and more with a RIO with a call sign of Boston. Boston went to a distinguished university and was planning on becoming an attorney when his tour with the Marines ended. He and his wife, along with Gene and Sue, became best friends with Susan and I.

In late 1971, while at Beaufort, it came to our attention that Fidel Castro was harassing an American shipping line for some reason. In response, the Warlords were given the mission to send eight F-4s down to Guantanamo Bay Cuba immediately. This deployment was to feature eight aircraft with good radars and live Aim-7 and Aim-9 Missiles. We responded quickly and I was chosen as one of the pilots to fly down to Cuba. We flew down and landed at Guantanamo. Only three times during the two weeks we were down there were we scrambled to intercept Cuban aircraft that were harassing boats of a foreign shipping company. We were pumped up to actually have live missiles and potentially be scrambled to intercept a real MIG adversary. However, all three times the MIGs left the area before we arrived and nothing happened.

The most memorable event that happened while I was in Guantanamo was that the Bob Hope Show came to the base. It was around the 1971 Christmas Holiday and Bob Hope was touring American military bases. Gene, Watchdog, Boston and I decided we were going to walk over and see the show. While walking to the show we were passed by double timing Marine platoons on their way to the show. They looked serious and they were impressive.

We watched the show and had a good time as did the whole crowd. Bob Hope did his comedy routines solo and then combined with different celebrity personalities including a group of Hollywood starlets called the Hollywood Debs. After the show we were walking back to our area and we were wearing our flight suits. Suddenly a jeep pulls up beside us and asked us if we were the crew that brought in the Bob Hope Show to Guantanamo. We told him we weren't and we were just Marine Pilots down here for an exercise.

"How would you like to go the Bob Hope After-Show party?" he asked. We looked at each other. We smiled and said, "Sure!"

While driving he introduced himself as Les Brown. We knew his name because he was famous as the leader of Les Brown and his Band Renown, which was known as Bob Hope's Band. We arrived at the party and started enjoying free drinks and snacks while we were introduced to astronaut Alan Shepard, singer and comedian Jim Nabors, country singer Charlie Pride, baseball pitcher Vida Blue and Bob Hope himself. Of course his accompanying group of beautiful ladies were also chatting with us. After an hour or two, Les gave us a ride back to our quarters. Wow, didn't see that coming. Must just be lucky.

During my second year at Beaufort, the Marine Corps decided it was time to put a Marine F-4 squadron back on a Navy Air Craft Carrier that was bound for Viet Nam. They selected our sister squadron VMFA-333 (Trip Trey). Suddenly VMFA-333 was getting special attention. They got all the extra parts. They received the best aircraft and radars. They got extra fuel so the aircrew could be up to speed to deploy onto the boat. The impact on VMFA-451 was devastating. I was no longer flying ten to fifteen hours a month but instead five to ten with practically no ACM. Our ping pong skills became formidable but our flight training was less impressive. We flew, worked out and went to the movies. I remember while waiting in line to see *The Godfather*, one of my Captain friends pulled out a little device, and we came to find out it was a battery powered calculator. It could add two plus two and come up with the right answer. We were dazzled. What would they invent next?

As it came closer to the time that pilots and RIOs would be sent to West Pac, they learned that they would have to attend

Marine Survival School. This school called for about ten officers to be trucked into the middle of the swamp in North Carolina. They issued each of us a topographical map, and we were told we would soon be tracked by Marine veteran Viet Nam ground pounders (grunts). If they caught us they would take us to a temporary POW (Prisoner Of War) camp where we would spend some time. Suddenly we heard gunfire, and our escort informed us we had one minute to begin evading the grunts that were approaching our position. We all took off running into the swamp country wearing just our military fatigues, t-shirts and flight boots. We broke apart like a bunch of quail, each of us determined not to be caught. I began to slow down and listen and almost immediately saw a grunt sitting on a log in front of me waiting for an officer to stumble into his position. I slowly and silently backtracked and took a different direction. Finding a good place to rest, I pulled out my map and tried to make sense of where I was and where I was trying to go.

After a couple more close calls I ran into another officer and we decided to team up. We talked it over and came to the agreement that the grunts were staying on the high ground. Therefore if we went down into the swamp water they would probably not be interested in looking for us there. North Carolina has rattlesnakes, copperheads and water moccasins. All very dangerous. The water moccasin is not only known for being dangerous, but also for being very aggressive. We saw several snakes, but fortunately for us it was winter, and the snakes appeared to be lethargic—as if in some form of hibernation. We covered ourselves with mud to both make us harder to see, and to keep the mosquitoes off us. After several hours we managed to make it to the rendezvous point without getting caught. That was unusual as most of the others had been caught.

Unfortunately, that did not keep us from being thrown into the POW camp. The camp was set up to train us to some extent to experience what being a POW might be like. The grunts were able to treat us rather roughly. For example they might take drum sticks and play the drums on your shins. Another trick was to tie a stick between your ankles keeping them spread which was incredibly uncomfortable. The worst "torture" was lowering an officer into a barrel of water headfirst and just holding them underwater by their ankles. That was very tough, and one officer had to go to the hospital after having a panic attack.

They also had a small metal box that would hold three men in a sitting position while holding their knees. You would be kept in there for a long period. Occasionally a new person would be put into the box, and he would attempt to start a conversation. We quickly figured out that this was a trick to get a person to say more than name, rank and serial number. Although we knew the grunts were not going to kill us it was serious enough to make us realize how difficult a POW environment could be.

Of course we were also taught how and when to fire a flare and how to use our signaling mirror as well as how to survive in the jungle. After the war I knew several former POWs and learned that what we had been introduced to at jungle survival school was helpful, but nothing like the actual thing.

Susan and I were now living in base housing, which was good. We had a dog, two cars and lots of friends. We got the opportunity to visit Savannah, Georgia and Charleston, North Carolina. Life was good, except for one thing: every month another two or three pilots and RIOs were being called up to go to Nam. Woody and Watchdog had already been given orders. In March, Gene was given his Orders. It was inevitable, but it was still a surprise when my Orders arrived, and in May of 1972 I was told to report to Seattle for transport to Travis Air Force Base in California. I was then to fly to Iwakuni, Japan, and then on to Cubic Point in the Philippines. From there I would fly to Da Nang, Viet Nam and join a fighter squadron. We decided that Susan would join her mother and father in Seattle while I was overseas. It was hopefully time for my training to begin to pay off.

Next stop Viet Nam and Combat!

CHAPTER FIVE

READY ROOM

To fully understand US Marine Corps fighter squadrons you must become acquainted with the Ready Room. A Ready Room is typically a room located above or near the aircraft maintenance hangar. It has to be large enough to hold a meeting with twenty to thirty aviators. On the walls are the plaques with squadron patches, lists of Commanding Officers, flight crews, deployments, and squadron awards. The wall would be covered with aircraft photos, deployment photos, safety rules, aircraft schematics, missiles, beautiful women, etc.

At the front of the Ready Room would be white boards for briefings and debriefings and a lectern. Four chairs are always in the front row. They often appear to be ejection seats. Each one has a marker clearly identifying for whom the seat is reserved. The Commanding Officer (CO), Executive Officer (XO), Operations Officer (OPSO) and Aviation Maintenance Officer (AMO) each have a designated chair. When a squadron is having an All Officer's Meeting (AOM) those chairs will not be used except by the Officers holding those titles. AOMs would be held at least weekly. There we would get talks from the NATOPs Officer and the Safety Officer. Often times the S-2 (Intelligence Officer) would do a briefing on adversary aircraft, missiles, anti-aircraft guns, etc. If

Ski (our Intelligence Officer) was doing the briefing we would always be looking at each other and asking,

"How does he know and remember all this stuff?"

The Scheduling Officer would go over the plan for the week, and the Ops O would talk about future deployments or special missions. Finally, the Skipper would introduce new members to the squadron and provide updates on our progress, hours, and future plans.

The room would have twenty or thirty comfortable leather chairs and a few leather couches. On one side of the room was the Scheduling Board holding the schedule for the flights and noting the pilots, RIOs, the aircraft number, as well as the type of mission to be flown that day. After hours, a Duty Officer would sit behind a counter with a row of phones. Oftentimes the counter had a glass case. In the case of the Death Rattlers squadron, it housed a live rattle snake.

Throughout the day and evening the Ready Room would be used for meetings, briefings, debriefings, training sessions and bull sessions. Marines would be in uniforms, flight suits or maybe civilian clothes, if just arriving or departing. If a flight was being briefed, there would be drawing on the chalk board and small model aircraft would be used as briefing aids. After the flights, again the board would be used to diagram and show what the perspective of the fight was from the different cockpits. There were always lots of discussions about who was shot first, or if you had died before you shot someone else.

This was a male dominated environment. It was not unusual to have loud belches. In fact one pilot, HJ, could belch loud enough and long enough that other conversations would stop in admiration. Guys would fart, and others would casually attempt to identify and name the offender, comment on the level of lethality, and perhaps ultimately move to better breathing areas.

Aircrew would sometimes make the mistake of falling asleep on one of the couches and would thereby immediately be branded as a target. Nothing was considered a higher form of humor than screwing with a fellow Marine to see if you could get a rise out of them.

This was an absolutely non-politically correct environment. This was true in every squadron around the world, not just in ours. Anything, everything, and anybody were targets for unfair criticism, insults and humor. The more you were liked and accepted, the more you were targeted. It was also expected that you would be able to take the jab and strike back effectively. Laughter and smiles were always involved. Crude language was common. I learned to have a mental switch that would turn on the course language if with the squadron and turn off if with my wife, family or civilians. This switch is still active today!

This was a dangerous job. People died doing it and shouldered the risk as acceptable. These were companions that you depended on and trusted with your life daily. They knew you in some ways better than anyone else in the world. Rank and position were respected when appropriate. The CO was typically addressed as Skipper. The XO was called the XO. Call Signs were predominantly used and were often colorful and well earned. Jumper earned his by being a world class high jumper. Grunt had previously served in Viet Nam as a platoon commander. Slim was slim and Casino was willing to take chances and fly on the edge. Slammer earned his call sign by being tossed in jail during one deployment while Frisco grew up in San Francisco. We had Pigs and Pork, Snoopy and Spud plus Fleet, Postal and Rookie, HJ, Killer and Dude. If you puked in your navigation bag you might become NavBag. Stories and legends were always about Call Signs. If I walked into the Officer's Club I expected not to be hailed as Greg but rather as Shadow.

This was also true in the air. While flying a conversation might sound like this:

"Lancer, break down hard port (left), Bogey at four o'clock low."

Lancer would respond

"Roger Shadow"

This would mean an adversary aircraft was approaching Lancer's aircraft from a four o'clock position below him and if he didn't break into the adversary immediately he would probably get a shot called on him. His response would typically come as he was physically starting to maneuver his aircraft acknowledging that he heard my call.

"Shadow, reverse starboard, I'm on his six!" Lancer might call out.

"Roger Lancer, and I'm approaching Bingo."

That would be a call from Lancer informing me that if I broke hard to the starboard (right) Lancer would be set up for an immediate kill shot on the adversary threatening me. My response acknowledged his plan and also told him that I was now at Bingo fuel state (pre-planned fuel state). When we reach this fuel state, it means the flight's over and we are bugging out.

The same type of conversation would be going on in the cockpit between pilot and RIO. The RIO was typically on the radar looking for bogeys at a distance, or if we were in a fight, his job was to keep our six clear and try to keep other aircraft in sight so we could avoid adversaries and help friends. They would also track altitude, airspeed, G's, and fuel state knowing that the pilot was fully engaged, looking outside the cockpit and concentrating on winning the fight and therefore might momentarily be less concerned with safety. An experienced pilot would typically have good situational awareness and would know what was going on in all domains, but a new pilot could be easily distracted.

If we were just flying between flights, then the conversations could and did cover every topic under the sun. Yes, we would be looking outside for other aircraft and keeping track of our navigation, but while flying with a good friend, it was sometimes easier to talk about some subjects without looking each other in the eye.

If a squadron mate died in the air, then the Ready Room would be where the Skipper would say a few remarks. That came after his first having to notify and mourn with the aircrew wives and family. Following this, shots of whiskey would be passed out to everyone. Then a toast, and a minute of silence would convey our shared sense of loss, and our respect.

Squadrons had a common theme: kill the enemy. The mission was to prepare to do that job effectively. Money didn't matter. Politics were trivial. Individual ambition was basically tuned toward attempting to fly better. Having a shared team mission is powerful. If you stayed in and didn't screw up too bad you would probably become a Captain and then a Major. After that point it became more selective. Squadron members changed constantly. You were always meeting and training the new people and saying goodbye to the departing folks.

The Ready Room was where you could completely be yourself. There you were surrounded by very competitive buddies focused on an extremely serious business, all the while being accepted and being trusted that you would do what needed to be done when it needed to be done. These were your buddies. Sharing funny stories and real problems were expected. You could say and do almost anything, and you were protected by the Code of Conduct that had only one rule: What happened in the squadron stayed within the squadron! Break that rule and you were gone.

I miss the Ready Room!

CHAPTER SIX

RIOs

Phantom Radar Intercept Officers (RIOs) were fearless and crazy. They went to a special Radar Intercept School and typically joined a Phantom squadron right out of that school. They were typically very smart, very confident and many had wanted to be pilots except they either didn't have the eyesight, or the pilot classes were already full. Either way they still wanted to fly. In order to hold their own in a squadron full of cocky fighter pilots, they had to put up with BS and dish it out. They had to command respect in the aircraft, if they were going to expect the pilot to listen to them. They had to be willing to fly with the best pilots and make them listen, and they had to fly with the worst pilots and help them survive.

They could pick out a radar target at thirty miles that to a pilot just looked like a little blob on the radar screen. That blob looked like every other blob. The good ones learned how to run a good intercept and then switch to looking out of the cockpit and track multiple aircraft. They could quickly determine priority risk/reward to their aircraft and their wingman, and make the quick concise radio calls to help both pilots take the right aggressive attack or evasive action. They constantly scanned the space to ensure their six o'clock was clear from bogey aircraft. They endured heavy five and six G turns when not expecting it. They experienced negative G's when not anticipating it. They watched altitudes, airspeeds, angles of attack, and fuel status when pilots were preoccupied with trying to get a shot.

They learned to navigate both domestically and internationally. They were typically the voice of the aircraft and flight to the outside world. They learned to help the pilot when bombing and typically tracked bombing success and anti-aircraft fire. They helped the Phantom pilot complete aerial refueling by talking them into the basket. They fired flares and chaff when under attack.

Most importantly they had control of the Command Eject Switch. If that switch was selected – ON, then if the RIO ejected, the pilot went too. This responsibility came with the definite possibility that the Pilot's ego might interfere with the decision to eject when trying to control an aircraft experiencing extreme problems. A RIO would focus on survival of both crew, while the pilot might be too busy trying to control the aircraft to initiate ejection.

Squadron RIOs really knew who they trusted as pilots. They flew with every pilot and could tell you what pilots were smooth and which ones were violent. Who could fly slow and who stayed calm under extreme pressure. They knew who got distracted, and which pilots were good when flying in the bad weather. They knew who they could trust regardless of circumstances and which pilots needed to be watched and subtly helped. Yet, even though they knew that flying with certain pilots was much more unpredictable and dangerous, they flew with them anyway. Imagine going straight up and running out of airspeed, or going straight at the ground at supersonic speeds with a pilot you know is not the best. That takes guts!

RIOs were squadron Commanding Officers, Executive Officers, Operations Officers and Maintenance Officers. In the Reserves, the pilots were often commercial airline pilots while the RIOs had more conventional jobs such as engineers, software developers, miners, aircraft engine consultants, solar engineers, entrepreneurs, etc. RIOs could be nerdy, brilliantly funny, extremely bright, loud, serious, and everything in between.

In short, an F-4 Phantom squadron is made up of pilots and RIOs. Pilots complain and make fun of RIOs, and RIOS complain and ridicule pilots. It is expected and welcomed. In the best squadrons the pilots and RIOs are often paired up. They become best friends and brothers. They laugh, argue, and complain, but are often found together. They know the other persons strengths and weakness both in the air and on the ground. They always have your back. They provide brutally honest critiques but also support when truly needed. The Phantom needed both to survive and both to excel. This bond was both unique, and essential, to the F-4 Phantom community.

God Bless RIOs! They saved me many times. I have nothing but respect for RIOs but for God's sake please don't tell them I said that.

PART TWO

Combat

CHAPTER SEVEN

RED DEVILS

Saying goodbye to family when one is going into a combat zone is not fun. In my case, the family accompanied me to the Seattle - Tacoma Airport where I would catch a plane going to Travis Air Force base in California.

My Dad was pretty quiet. He had flown B-29 bomber missions out of Saipan over Japan in WWII. He had lost friends during those missions. At one time his aircraft had been so damaged after dropping his bombs that he had been forced to divert and land on Iwo Jima. Upon landing, his aircraft had been surrounded by U.S. Marines. These Marines informed the crew that the Japanese were very active at night, and they would love to take out his B-29. They suggested that the crew abandon the aircraft and join them in the trenches. My Dad told the Marines that his crew would stay aboard and protect the aircraft, but also warned the Marines to not approach the aircraft, because his crew would fire at anything that moved. The B-29 Super Fortress featured 8 fifty caliber machine gun turrets firing with an advanced fire control system, and 1 twenty millimeter cannon in the rear. In other words, that single aircraft had multiple high powered machine guns. The Marines listened and stayed away. The Japanese were not so smart.

So, as he said goodbye, Dad knew it was the ultimate test. On one hand, he was proud. On the other hand, he knew the risk and the possibility that he would lose his oldest son. He just shook my hand, gave me a hug, and said "I'm proud of you! Come back!"

Mom was typically pretty calm and always wore lots of smiles. On this particular day, however, she was not smiling. Instead, she just kept grabbing my hand and squeezing it, her sentiments readily reflected by the tears in her eyes. She kissed me and simply said "I Love You!"

Susan was also very quiet. She had been expecting this for months. While she had seen how other wives handled these types of goodbyes, it was now our turn for goodbye as well.

The one thing I did not want to do was tear-up. I was a Marine going into combat. However, try as I did, I failed. I couldn't keep dry-eyed. One last hug and kiss, and we both said, "I love you!" to each other.

I turned and walked onto the commercial aircraft.

The next thing I remembered is landing at Da Nang Marine Air Base in Viet Nam on June 5th, 1972. As we were taxiing in to park, I saw rows of F-4 Phantoms. Some were parked in big revetments. A revetment was a place to park an aircraft with three sided blast walls, or sometimes half domes of concrete that an aircraft could taxi into for the purpose of then being loaded up with bombs and missiles. The idea here was that in the case of a rocket or bomb attack where a single aircraft was hit, it would not take out the rest of the flight line.

Despite the impressive rows of Phantoms, however, what really got my attention was an Air Force C-41 transport aircraft that was being loaded. Sitting beside the aircraft were row after row of caskets with American Flags draped over each one. Those were Americans going home. That could not have been more sobering. I was in a war zone.

We unloaded off the aircraft and were assigned to a jeep that would take us to our assigned squadron. On the way I noticed some Marines jogging, and one of them stood out to me. He had a very distinctive run that I remembered from my Washington State University high jumping days. More about that later.

I checked into my squadron, the VMFA-232 Red Devils. This F-4 Phantom squadron was flying the advanced but heavier F-4J. Our sister squadron was the VMFA-115 Silver Eagles, flying the F-4B.

I was so relieved to run into Gene, and as soon as I got out of my Jeep he took me on a tour. I was to sleep in a tin covered hooch with five other Marine flyers. A Hooch was slang for what was our primitive and shared living area. Definitely not extravagant, but suitable for the purpose. The first thing Gene had me do was go outside and drag in a metal door and put that under my mattress. He then instructed me that in the case of a rocket attack I should roll out of my bed and get under the bed. I soon ran into Woody and Watchdog. I was also introduced to a bunch of guys who had joined VMFA-232 from the Hawaii squadrons. I met the Commanding Officer and Executive Officer and Operations Officer. Each asked me questions and gave me a short briefing.

They told me to get settled and I would start flying soon. One week later I was to go up on my first flight with Woody, the flight lead, and it was just to get used to the flight line, the arming stations, taxi ways, and to also do a takeoff and landing. I would also get to scope out the area a little to see the air base and the surrounding country. Meanwhile, I was assigned my flight suit, helmet, my G-suit, my flotation harness and my safety harness. The safety harness was critical. It included a map covered in plastic, a couple of small water bottles, a whistle, a small paper with some Vietnamese words on it to hopefully ask people to help me if I was shot down. It included a small mirror to flash at aircraft from the ground, a flare gun, an emergency locator beacon, and a radio. You then got to select a pistol. The choices were a forty five caliber or a thirty eight caliber. I had qualified as an expert with the Smith and Wesson thirty eight and I liked the fact that it was light, so that was my choice.

Did I mention that it was hot (in the 90s) and very humid? Walking out to the aircraft on a huge concrete tarmac surrounded by jet engines and machinery while wearing a flight suit and a G-suit and safety harness was hot. While climbing into the cockpit you realized that it was now suddenly even hotter. You had to lower the canopy before getting airborne and before the cooling system starting working. Words cannot describe just how unmercifully hot it was. I would sweat so bad my flight gloves were wet. In twelve months in Viet Nam I don't remember ever being cold.

The first flight was calm, and I found that the area around Da Nang was truly beautiful. The landing was uneventful and I was subsequently declared combat ready. My flight the next day was to be an early morning flight. My first combat flight was the next day, June 14th, 1972.

This was the daily routine for the next twelve months. You would hear the bugle and you are to get up and go to the mess hall for breakfast. The food was always good, but nothing fancy. Next, you would attend your flight briefing. This is where you'd find out who your flight crews were to be that day. Since I was a pilot I would find out who my RIO would be. We discovered who would lead the flight and who would be the lead RIO. By the way, when you became qualified you were typically crewed up with a Pilot or RIO that you fly with almost every flight. Everyone liked that.

Would we be two aircraft (Section) or four aircraft (Division)? This is where they tell you what type of mission you would be flying, who you would be contacting for aerial refueling, and where it should occur. Would you have a rendezvous with Navy aircraft or Air Force Aircraft? Would you be working with a Forward Air Controller (FAC) on the ground or airborne? Perhaps most important of all would be what type of armament you'd be carrying. How many Sparrow-7 (Radar) missiles? How many Aim-9 (Sidewinder) heat seeking missiles. How many bombs? Are they two hundred and fifty pounds? Are they five hundred pounds or one thousand pounds? Do I have any five inch Zuni Rockets? Does my armament include CBUs (Cluster Bomb Units)? Napalm? What type of fuses are set on the bombs? You may have a fuse that goes off when the bomb hits the ground or you may have a bomb with a thirty inch fuse so that when the bomb hits it explodes and wipes out anything that may be walking. That type of bomb is known as the "Daisy Cutter."

This information is critical. For example, if your ordinance is Napalm, you know you will be supporting ground troops and you will be flying very low and relatively slow (four hundred knots). By the way, one hundred knots is equal to about one hundred fifteen miles per hour so four hundred knots was about four hundred sixty miles per hour. This would be an important but dangerous mission.

Next, you go into a weather briefing where a meteorologist provides you with the best guess for what type of cloud cover, wind strength, and direction that you should expect for takeoff, over the target, and upon returning to land.

For the last order of business, you go into the most important briefing, and that is to learn the details on your target and the likely anti-aircraft weapons you might encounter during this mission. If it is a bombing mission, you are told the general target area you would be hitting. This is critical. Certain areas were known to be heavily defended. An aircraft might have been shot down the previous day. You could feel the tension in the room ratchet up or down depending on the target. You would be told if that target had SA-2 or SA-6 missiles. Would it be likely to have fifty-seven millimeter or ZSU-23-4? Have SA-7s been fired in the area? Each of these would result in a different strategy. For example, a target defended with a Fifty-Seven MM meant they could be firing a single barrel with two hundred rounds a minute at you when you were at fifteen thousand feet circling the target. Not advanced technology, but good to know. On the other hand, a ZSU-23-4 Shilka was a four barrel, self-propelled 23MM cannon that could fire eight hundred to one thousand rounds a minute up to an altitude of nine thousand feet. They were accurate and lethal with advanced radar guided fire control systems. We hated to hear a ZSU-23-4 might be in the target area.

SA-2 were surface-to-air (SAM) Missiles that were as big as telephone poles and would be going twice the speed of sound when fired at you, but featured older technology and if spotted could be avoided. The SA-6 (Gainful) was a highly advanced radar guided missile system with smaller, very fast missiles that were very difficult to see when airborne. Again, this was a weapon system you did not want to face.

If the target featured ZSU-23-4 or SA-6 missile defense systems, everybody was wide awake. We had systems in our aircraft called RAWH gear that could tell you when an enemy system was watching you, tracking you, or firing at you. The gear featured a small screen on the right side of the cockpit that would show one type of signal if a radar was generally watching you. If the radar/missile system began tracking you, another signal would indicate from where the tracking was occurring, and would give the crew an audio signal. When and if the missile actually was fired at you, then the RAWH gear would sound an alarm and indicate where you should look to try to find a visual on the missile. Once visually identified, your goal was to wait and judge when to make a high G turn (4-5 Gs) into the missile so that it overshot and missed you before exploding. Imagine knowing a supersonic telephone pole with dynamite has been fired specifically at you. That might give you some idea of the level of attention that went into defeating the approaching missile.

Of course, our systems would try to defeat their radar. The Phantom RIO could deploy chaff from our Phantoms to try to confuse tracking radars. The Phantom also had flares that could be fired to defeat tracking heat seeking missiles. Or, if we had the right aircraft in our flight (Wild Weasels), if an enemy radar system came up and started tracking the good guys they would lock on the enemy radar and blow it up. Unfortunately, having access to Wild Weasels on a daily basis was very unusual. So that meant the following: If the target had advanced defenses, it meant the bombing runs would be a single run, where you would drop all the bombs at a higher altitude and then run for your life. If the target did not purport to have advanced defenses, then the flights may make more bombing runs and fly a little lower to ensure the targets were hit.

Following the briefings, it was now time to go out to the locker room and put on the flight gear, grab your helmet, and visit the maintenance shed. The maintenance shed is where you will find out what aircraft you have been assigned, and where you will look through the maintenance log to see what type of issues the individual aircraft might expect to exhibit. For example, the aircraft might have a great radar or a poor radar.

You would now walk out into the heat and the noise and inspect your aircraft and the loaded ordinance. Finally, it was time to climb into the aircraft. Start the two huge jet engines and begin to feel the power that the Phantom exudes. Your plane captain would walk you thru a number of checks and finally he would remove the chocks, he would salute and you'd salute back, and then you'd roll out of the flight line. You'd then head over to one of the revetments. There the ordinance crew takes over. They inspect all the missiles and bombs. They would remove the safety pins on the bombs so now the bombs were live. A typical load in Viet Nam was (two) Sparrows, (two) sidewinders, (two) Zuni rockets, and (twelve) five hundred pound bombs. The ordinance Chief pulls the chocks, gives a thumbs up and salutes you as you salute him back. You would goose the engines to pull onto the Taxiway and proceed to the end of the runway.

At the end of the runway you run your engines up to military power and verify all the gauges look good. You give a thumbs up to the flight lead and wait for clearance for takeoff.

When it is your turn to take off, you'd run the power up to military and then engage the afterburners.The afterburners on the F-4 push the thrust up to eighteen thousand pounds per engine and the impact is always a thrill, but when you have a combat load of fuel and bombs it takes a while to get airborne. Once in the air, you raise the landing gear, the flaps, and disengage afterburner. The combat flight has begun.

After takeoff we would join up with our flight lead and inspect his aircraft, looking closely at the ordnance they were carrying. Then we would switch leads and they'd inspect our aircraft. With no noted issues, we would begin climbing up to altitude while talking with a combat controller who'd directs us toward our target area. Once we got close we would be directed to change frequencies and begin speaking with our Forward Air Controller (FAC). Typically in Nam when you arrive on station you are directed to orbit at altitude while the FAC works with another flight that has arrived before you.

This FAC briefing was important as you learned several things. First, you learned what type of target you might be hitting. Was it a structure, a tank, a bridge, troops, or something else? Second, you paid attention to the wind direction. To highlight a target, a FAC would fire a phosphorus rocket (Willey Pete) that would smoke when it hit the ground. Then he might direct you to hit one klick (thousand meters) to the north of the smoke or maybe hit one hundred meters south of the smoke or occasionally hit the smoke. That is when you could actually see what the target might be. Third, and most important, you could see what type of ground fire the American aircraft were experiencing while in their runs. If it looked like sparkling lights on the ground then that was likely North Vietnamese firing their rifles at the aircraft. If there was grey and white explosions near the aircraft in their runs, then you knew they had serious anti-aircraft guns. Oftentimes the FAC would tell an aircraft that was pulling off the target that a SA-7 had been fired at them. The SA-7 was a shoulder mounted heat seeking missile that the ground troops would fire at your aircraft.

Finally the FAC would start talking to your flight. In the cockpit it would be time to start flicking the arming switches on. The FAC would shoot his Willey Pete and give you the direction to roll in from and the target distance from the smoke.

In the Phantom we had three standard dive angles: ten degrees, thirty degrees and forty five degrees. The most common was a thirty degree bombing run. In a thirty degree bombing run you would wait until the target was at your low three o'clock and then pull the nose down right and begin a thirty degree dive towards the target. In the cockpit things began happening very fast. The pilot would be trying to put his bombing site reticle below the target while figuring out what effect the wind would have on the bomb flight. If you had a cross wind from the right you would have to aim off the target to the right. If the wind was behind you the reticle would have to be put short of the target and if you had a headwind you had to put it slightly beyond the target. Meanwhile your RIO is yelling out your airspeed and altitude. In a perfect run there would be no wind. You would be at four hundred and fifty knots precisely and you would release the bombs at exactly the right altitude just as your reticle was over the target. Of course, that never happened! You would be too slow or too fast. You might be too shallow or too steep. And meanwhile you would be jinxing the aircraft left and right so the gunners on the ground did not have a steady target. Also you would see the sparkling on the ground and explosions in the air around you. You had to make accommodations for variations on just about every bombing run.

You would release the bombs and immediately begin a four to five G pullout while again jinxing while looking back to see the impact of your bombs on the target. At the same time the next aircraft has begun his run on the target. If you were told a SA-7 had been fired at your aircraft, you would pull into the direction of the missile, come out of afterburner, and fire flares out of the side of your aircraft hoping that the heat seeking missile would home in on the hot flares rather than your engines. Once you were away from the target you would pull back up to altitude. Maybe you make another run or two if the target defenses are minimal. If not then you join with your flight lead and check each other for any hits or damage. Then we climb back up to a safe altitude and head back to the base.

A forty five degree bombing run felt very steep and fast. You would release the bomb at a higher altitude so it was less accurate but in a highly dangerous target area the forty five degree run was preferred. The ten degree run was typically only used when American troops were in trouble and had called for close air support.

A ten degree bombing run was very accurate because you would be flying close to the ground and relatively slow (four hundred knots) but that also meant that you were a much easier target for the ground fire. Generally you would be carrying napalm or cluster bomb units (CBUs). CBUs were bombs that when dropped would open like a clam shell and drop hundreds of small bombs like powerful grenades over the enemy position. You knew if you were called to a mission with Napalm it was very serious and you knew the American troops were engaged with the Viet Cong in a close combat situation. That meant you had to come in low and close over the American troop position and drop your munitions on the enemy without dropping any on the American troops. It had to be precise, accurate bombing. But that also meant you would be flying low and slow right over the enemy position. Of course, hopefully the enemy would be diving into a ditch to avoid what you had just dropped on their heads.

It was always a great feeling to be in a bar in Viet Nam and have some of the Marine grunts notice you in your flight suit, come over, and ask what you flew. They loved the Phantoms and always expressed what it meant to them to have close air support when they really needed it.

One time my RIO Boston and I were in a three aircraft bombing mission. My best friend Gene was in one of the aircraft. The target was in a relatively safe area. We saw the flights ahead of us take no observable ground fire. We decided to make single bomb runs where each aircraft would make six runs in total. Our FAC was a real cheerleader. After each bombing run he would cheer how close the bomb hit and exclaim how amazing we were doing. Wow, we were really good and this was fun!

Near our last run I heard Gene pull out and call over the radio that they had been hit. What? They had been hit? They climbed up to altitude and we joined up to look them over. I was shocked at the damage. They had lost some of their stabilator and about half their rudder. They also had some damage to the wing flaps. This was serious. The stabilator is what controls the up and down motion of the aircraft. The rudder moves the nose of the aircraft from side to side and allows you to steer at high speed on the runway. The wing flaps allow you to slow down to a safe landing speed. The aircraft was flying OK now but when it got slower would Gene be able to control the nose? When they landed would he be able to steer the aircraft on the runway without a rudder? Because of the damage to the flaps we advised him not to lower the flaps which meant he would be making a high speed landing.

We called Da Nang and declared an emergency and told the ground crews the status of Gene's aircraft. We were instructed to make a straight in approach and landing, and that I should land first in case they had a problem on the runway with Gene. It was tough to give Gene a thumbs up and accelerate ahead of him in order to land. I was furious that we had been so stupid as to make so many bombing runs. But I was mostly worried that my best friend was in this situation.

When we landed the entire air base was at a standstill. The taxi ways were clear. No aircraft or ground machinery was moving. Everyone on the base had seen the emergency vehicles sirens and knew a damaged aircraft was coming in to attempt a landing. We pulled off the runway and looked back as Gene's aircraft came in hot and landed OK but was eating up available runway quickly. His drag chute was deployed and then he dropped it so it wouldn't affect the nose of his aircraft. The brakes were smoking as he stopped the aircraft and turned off the runway. We met them on the flight line. I gave Gene a big handshake and put my arm over his shoulder as we walked. He just shook his head, grinned and said,

"Well, that was exciting!

Da Nang Airbase in 1972 was large, brown, filled with Marines, bombs, fuel dumps, revetments, aircraft of all types and it was humming with activity. We would typically fly one or two sorties a day. There was an Officers Club where you could get a beer. It was rare to go off base. Stories were told of vans filled with Marines with someone running along the side of the van and dropping a grenade inside. I don't know if it was true or false but it was safer on the base. At night we would sometimes hear the beginning of a rocket attack. It would be a far off whoompf sound and then every few seconds the sounds would get softer or louder. If louder then we knew the rockets were being walked in our direction. Some evenings we would see a Spectre AC-130 Gun Ship circling the base. These gun ships were the large propeller driven cargo C-130s with special outfitting including three powerful guns: the 25mm Gatling gun, (called the Crowd pleaser) three hundred twenty five rounds a minute, the 45 mm Bofors Cannon firing two hundred rounds a minute and the 105mm Howitzer firing ten rounds a minute. The gunships would circle the perimeter of the base with their infrared capability and when they would spot enemy targets they would open up with both the Crowd Pleaser and the Bofars cannon at the same time. Every fifth round is a red tracer round so you can see where your rounds are going. With both guns going it would look like a red laser line going down to the target with a very familiar mechanical machine gun sound. We would look at each other, shake our heads and say, "Boy I'm glad they are not shooting at me!"

After less than a month in Da Nang, the entire Marine Air Wing relocated to Nam Phong, Thailand in late June. The Air Force had built a twelve thousand foot long emergency landing runway in Nam Phong in case a B-52 had to make an emergency landing while returning from missions over Vietnam. The Marine Air Wing arrived with two F-4 Phantom Squadrons, an A-6 Intruder squadron, a couple of C-130 tanker aircraft and a few choppers. When we first arrived they put all the Marines into the large, aluminum, aircraft maintenance hangers. Each Marine had a cot with mosquito netting, and one foot locker. There was no air conditioning, limited fans, limited outdoor latrines, and limited showers. There was a large tent for chow and tents for flight briefing. It was extremely hot and humid. If while sleeping your arm fell outside the mosquito netting you would have mosquito bites up and down your arm. There was little to do except fly the missions, do your secondary job and sit on your cot and think about how thirsty you were.

At that time there was a popular country song by Lynn Anderson called "I Never Promised You a Rose Garden". Not long after the song was released, along came a Marine recruiting poster showing a stern Marine Drill Instructor a couple of inches away from a young recruit. The text read, "We don't promise you a rose garden. The Marines are looking for a few good men!" Soon the Nam Phong Marine base was simply known as "The Rose Garden."

Because the shower facilities were still being built there is one sight I will never forget. When it would rain for a few minutes you would suddenly have hundreds of Marines stripping off their clothes and running to get under the water pouring down off the aluminum aircraft hangar roofs. Soaping up and yelling and laughing hoping the rain would last long enough to get all the soap off. Women would have loved to have had their cameras.

Gradually the base took shape. The two F-4 Phantom gun squadron air crews were put into wooden structures covered by canvas tents. Each hooch carried six aircrew with cots, mosquito netting, and foot lockers. Large canvas pools of non-potable water were at the end of the row of hooches. When it was time for a shower you would carry a large bowl down to the water with a towel and soap. You would pour water over yourself, soap down and rinse. Then take a bowl full of water back to the hooch so you could set up your mirror on a shelf and shave. Over time each hooch built also had a little deck in front.

The latrines were six-hole latrines about thirty yards away from the hooches. They were disgusting in every way you can imagine. The latrines were simply small rectangular sheds with screening so you could look out. The latrine featured two benches opposite each other with three diamond holes cut out of each bench. Beneath each hole was a barrel. It was common to use the latrines at night when maybe you would be the only one using the latrine. The sounds and smells encountered in those latrines were something I would never like to experience again.

There were only two air conditioned spaces on the base. The General's quarters and the Barber shop. It was a common practice to go get a haircut once a week. This was because once you were one of the final three waiting for your haircut you got to move inside the air conditioned space. When it was your turn the barber would buzz around your head for a while. When he was finished you would step outside into the blast furnace again. When not flying, each Officer also had a secondary job. Mine was in Aircraft Maintenance and the Quality Control Shop. I had a Staff Sergeant that knew everything and took care of everything. I tried to learn and help. What I really learned was just how much pride the troops had in keeping the aircraft in an UP status and to make sure the aircrew returned safely after every mission. They would work round the clock in extremely hot and humid conditions to make sure no aircraft was down because of their department.

At night, after all the flights were down and the maintenance shift was over, we would drift over to the mess hall and grab some chow and then wander back to our hooches. Sometimes we played combat volleyball or football. Once a week we might roll out the projector and watch a movie on a sheet hanging down from a tree. Most of us got letters from our family and friends. The letters from Susan always had perfume and were a reminder of home. Most of us had cassette players where we could play some music. I had six tapes that I played endlessly. Otherwise we just sat around in our shorts, because it was always hot, and talked about everything... and nothing.

Maybe once every couple of months we would get an R&R and could take a bus to the nearest town. They would have lots of bars and restaurants especially targeting the US military men in the area. The bars featured excellent bands singing American music. Also found were massage parlors and lots of hookers. It was always such a relief to not be in a uniform, and be able to sit in an air conditioned bar and have attractive young women trying to get your attention.

One time we were getting a ride off the base to where the bus would pick us up for our ride to the town. The truck we were on was dedicated to picking up the barrels that had been in the latrines and taking them out to a place to be dumped. The smell was a stench I could not believe. Then the driver said something amazing. He found out we were pilots and said,

"I wouldn't do what you do for anything!"

Gene and I just looked at each other and shook our heads and grinned.

Another time we went to the Udorn Air Force Base that was supporting F-4s and other aircraft involved in the war. I was with Boston, Cal, and another pilot, Eagle. We began having a few drinks. I knew that whenever Cal started drinking he got very aggressive and almost looked for fights. It became my unofficial job to keep an eye on Cal and make sure he didn't get into much trouble. After too many drinks we approached the Officer's Club and I decided that I could be aggressive too. I kicked the front door to begin opening it. To my dismay my foot went right through the door and now the door had a twelve inch panel missing. We turned around and scooted out of there before anybody could recognize us.

Because The Rose Garden was in central Thailand it had a dramatic effect on the missions. The aircraft would be outfitted with the same armament, but always a minimum of one centerline fuel tank. That one centerline fuel tank, along with the distance to the target itself, meant that aerial refueling would be required on every mission.

Aerial refueling on a C-130 was an interesting task. The C-130 is not a fast aircraft. To refuel, the Phantom would have to be slowed to around two hundred and twenty knots. You would also need to be leveled off at about twenty thousand feet. The F-4 had a refueling probe that would be extended beside the RIO's canopy. It extended a few feet. The C-130 would trail two refueling drogues which were small baskets at the end of hoses trailing twenty or thirty feet behind and below each wing.

The challenge was to contact the tanker, get a tally ho (a visual sighting), join on the tanker's wing, and get clearance to begin refueling. That is when the competition would begin. The challenge was to drop behind the basket and move slowly forward until you could put the probe into the basket and start receiving fuel. The proper way to complete this maneuver was to have your RIO talk you into position while the pilot looked straight ahead. Because the refueling probe nozzle was right next to the pilot's head, it was easy to start fencing with the basket if the pilot attempted to refuel on his own. Of course, if you were good and experienced, the pilot knew where the probe was and could complete the maneuver without help. The goal was to be the first to plug AND to plug on the first attempt. Anything less was a competitive failure and you would hear about it during the debriefing or at the bar. What made this maneuver more difficult during Viet Nam was that your aircraft had a full, heavy bomb load and when you added a full fuel load the Phantom became sluggish and not far from stall speed. Real embarrassment and danger came if the basket was torn loose and stayed on the probe, or if the refueling probe was damaged.

The distance from Nam Phong to Da Nang was just under five hundred miles. So after refueling, the flight would fly east until crossing into Viet Nam and then we'd began speaking with the Combat controllers in order to be sent over to the right radio channel for your FAC to receive initial target direction and information. Many times the flight would take off, refuel, fly over to Viet Nam, find the target, hit the target, luckily experience minimal ground to air fire, refuel again if necessary, and return to Nam Phong. On the way back we would be thrilled to be alive. We might fly a little ACM or just fly low and look at the countryside. When we flew ACM, I soon learned that the crews that had come out of Hawaii or the west coast, were much better than me. In August I became a Captain and was leading missions on a daily basis.

Sometimes things got exciting. On one mission we were to hit a target near Hue, which was always bad news. We were cleared into the target area and began circling at high altitude, around 17,000 feet, watching the aircraft below us go after the target. This was typical and considered pretty safe as no SAMs were in the area. We were circling and I glanced back at my wingman who was a couple of miles behind me and across the circle. I was shocked to see grey and black explosions right behind his aircraft at his altitude. I jumped on to the radio and told my wingman to dive and check his six. He immediately did and the explosions stopped. We knew a 57 MM anti-aircraft gun had found his altitude and from that moment on I was always more disciplined about changing altitude when orbiting a target.

Another time we were up North, closer to the North Viet Nam border. It was not a favorable target area with too many bad guys on the ground with good anti-aircraft resources. Friendly aircraft had been shot down there recently.

The FAC told us our target and said forty five degree bombing runs. Only one run per aircraft. OK. We lowered down to our orbit level and commenced our dive. We approached our release altitude at five hundred knots and just when I pickled off the bombs, I heard an explosion. It was deafening in the cockpit. I was pulling off the target and jinxing like a madman. In addition, I was pulling G's and scanning my instruments to see if we were losing fuel or hydraulics or an engine.

I tried to talk with my RIO, Boston, but he was silent. Has he been hit? Has he ejected? What is going on? I was keeping my airspeed up and trying to get away from the target area while asking my wingman to join up with me and tell me what he saw. He managed to join up and proceeded to inform me that the rear canopy was gone, but Boston was still in the aircraft. He was hunkered down as low as he could get. Well that made sense, because we were going five hundred knots, and if he got his head or an arm into the slip stream he would lose it! I slowed down to two hundred knots and I was looking in my mirrors and I saw a thumbs up from Boston. I'm wasn't sure his oxygen mask was OK. I knew the cockpit was no longer pressurized. It means I have to fly lower and slower, but we were still over the bad guys. We hoped Boston's ejection seat didn't fire off. We made it back to Da Nang and landed without further incident.

Once when flying out of Da Nang, I was assigned a bombing mission. We were to join up on a Navy Aircraft utilizing a sophisticated LORAN system along with some other Navy aircraft and drop bombs on a target fairly close to Da Nang. The Navy aircraft would lead the mission and when they directed us we would release our load of twelve five hundred pound bombs. We managed to find and join up with the Navy aircraft. I was flying close formation in clouds but wanting to know where we were. I stole a quick glance at my TACAN navigation gauge. It was spinning. I knew the Navy pilot would be using his Inertial Navigation system, which were very accurate, so I was not worried. The Navy pilot told us to arm our bombs and began a countdown. At his call I pickled our bomb load. Shortly after the release we heard a call from Da Nang on the Emergency channel informing us that Da Nang was under attack and all approaching aircraft were to go into a holding pattern until the attack was confirmed over and the runway had been cleared.

After about ten minutes Da Nang was declared open and we jumped into the approach pattern and made a landing while the Navy pilot returned to his base and the Navy aircraft returned to their air craft carrier. We taxied into the flight line parking area and were met by the Plane Captain who described the attack. He then held up a fragment that he had picked up after the attack. I looked at it and realized it looked like a piece of the outer layer of a bomb that we typically dropped. Later that evening we were told that Da Nang had indeed been bombed by its own aircraft. The next day I had to meet with our squadron skipper and found out it had been our flight. It turned out the Navy pilot had mistakenly put Base coordinates rather than the Target coordinates in his LORAN targeting system.

Eventually we were not held accountable because our TACAN's were spinning so there was no way we could know how far out from Da Nang we were bombing. Luckily there were no deaths or casualties as a result of the bomb drop. Sheesh! I had bombed Da Nang!

Sometimes after a mission, rather than flying back to the Rose Garden, we would go land at Da Nang, refuel, and get another load of bombs and fly another mission. Occasionally we would be told to shut the aircraft down and informed we would be spending the night in Da Nang at the BOQ (Bachelor Officer Quarters). That was OK with us. Actual buildings with beds and air conditioning sounded good.

One time we were spending the night and were bunking in a room that had four bunk beds. There was a salty, Warrant Officer that had been in Da Nang forever. We asked him what the plan was if we had a rocket attack that night. He laughed but said:

"Don't worry but...if you see me get up during an attack then get up and haul ass behind me."

Great! We went to sleep and I was awakened by the distant sound... a soft whoompf sound. Then the whoompf sound got louder, then louder and suddenly the Warrant Officer jumped out of bed in his shorts and hauled ass out of the room. We jumped out of our bed and scurried after him. He was moving quickly between buildings while the whoompf sound was growing louder. He suddenly disappeared into what looks to be a dumpster set on its side surrounded by sand bags. We got inside, sat down and looked at each other in our skivvies and laughed. Suddenly the whoompf sound was very close and the laughter stopped. The next whoompf sound hit and I found myself down on the floor compressed into the smallest ball I could make and was negotiating deals with God if he would just save my life. The next whoompf hit and it is the loudest noise I had ever heard and the dumpster shook a little and then the sound was going away from us. After a few minutes, the Warrant Officer got up and we wandered back to our room. All he says is, "Well, that one was pretty close."

The noise was so loud and I felt so helpless just lying there in the dumpster wondering if we would be hit. After that event I felt even more respect for the Grunts that were living out in the bush and having incoming rocket attacks as a common occurrence.

Another time we were airborne up North and close to the border again. We were making a thirty degree bombing run and the ground was just covered with red sparkles. I know we were being shot at... a lot. As we pulled off the target our FAC says, "Motion 20 you have one SA-7 fired at you! Then he says, "No make that two, no make it three SA-7s."

We were now flying very low and pulling G's but not with afterburner because SA-7s are heat seeking missiles. Then the FAC says, "Motion 20 they have fired seven SA-7s at you, continue jinking."

What? Seven SA-7s. Seriously? We see two and never see the rest. They miss us. We head home.

Once we were on a mission up in Laos. It was not a target we had ever approached before and it looked pretty quiet. We were the first flight on target. The FAC laid down a smoke and told us to hit the side of this hill close to the smoke. Our lead, Eagle, rolled in and I expected nothing, but looked to see how his bombs hit. Suddenly, while they were in the bombing run, it looked like the whole hillside opened up with big red and white sparkled firing and Eagle's aircraft was hidden by white and grey explosions. It looked like a WWII bombing run and I was amazed and relieved when I saw Eagle pulling off target and jinking away successfully. That is when my relief ended, as I realized we were next!

I have to tell you it was one of those times when the last thing I wanted to do was go into a bombing run on that target. What were we going to bomb that was worth our lives? I did not want to do it! But...next thing I know we are rolling into our dive. I fired a couple of Zuni rockets hoping to keep their heads down. It did not work. Again it looked like the entire hill was opening up with not little sparkles but now big sparkles. In front of us and beside us I saw countless explosions and knew people on the ground were seriously trying to kill us and they were getting very close to accomplishing that mission. We released the bombs and jinked like crazy. We joined up with Eagle and saw neither aircraft had been hit.

Have I mentioned that I've always been lucky?

By the way, when people later in my life ask about my Viet Nam experience they sometimes ask if I feel any guilt. I say that after many years I had learned what a mess the politics really were... but at that time all I knew were that people were trying to kill me and my friends every single day and sometimes they were succeeding. No, I felt no guilt.

Of course, not everyone was as lucky as me. During early November a pilot, Sam Cordova, and I were on R&R in Da Nang. We went out to the beach and it was spectacular with great sand and picturesque islands. We had a great day and talked about how after the war what a great vacation beach this would make. Well, the next month, while on a mission, Sam and his RIO, Arnie (who was one of my hooch mates), were hit and had to eject. While floating down in the chutes Sam started speaking on his emergency radio. He could see Arnie, in his chute close by but Arnie said nothing on his radio. They went down into the jungle.

When an American aircraft went down in Viet Nam it triggered lots of action. Immediately every aircraft in the area was sent over and put under control of the FAC so that the bombing intensity would increase, hopefully keeping Viet Cong search parties from venturing out looking for the crews. Also a Jolly Green Sikorsky HH-3 Helicopter would be scrambled and start flying to where the aircrew went down. Sam was speaking to the FAC and telling him that he was on the ground and OK. No visual or contact with Arnie yet. Also, Sam told the FAC that he could hear the Viet Cong on the hill below him and they sounded like they were getting closer.

The Jolly Green Giant arrived and picked up Sam's emergency beacon and headed for the hill where he was hiding. They got over his hill and Sam said he could see the Jolly Green right above him. They lowered the cable with the jungle penetrator (a metal device to penetrate the jungle canopy but with arms that could be unfolded to sit on while the cable was pulled in). As soon as the cable was lowered the Jolly Green started taking heavy ground fire. They told Sam to get on the device because they had to lift out of that area or get shot down themselves. The Jolly Green lifted up and began to egress. Suddenly out of the top of the trees appeared a body hooked on to the penetrator cable by a D-ring but not seated on the device. They pulled the cable up and helped the Marine into the chopper. That was when they realized the Marine was Arnie not Sam. Evidently Arnie's radio did not work and all he knew was suddenly a penetrator and cable landed above him on the hill and skidded down the hill beside him. He ran over and just barely hooked his D-ring to the cable before it started to pull him up through the jungle tree branches. Sam was never heard from again nor found.

Whenever I visit the very moving and emotionally draining Viet Nam Memorial Wall in Washington D.C. I look for and visit Sam. Even today, close to fifty years after the end of the Viet Nam War, people still visit the powerful memorial because every life that was lost can be found on that wall. They leave mementos, notes, photos of kids they never saw grow up, flowers, and then they hang their heads... and it is very quiet along the entire Wall.

Of course we had rudimentary Rose Garden Bars. There were three bars. The Enlisted Bar, The NCO Bar, and the Officer's bar. The Officer's Bar was a tent set off from the rest of the Officer's tents. It was simply a counter with booze behind it and a few tables where the aircrew could gather and blow off steam. Each of the Squadrons had special colorful jump suits made in the colors of the squadron. The Red Devil's was bright red with white stripes down the legs. Patches would be displayed. For example, for each hundred missions you would add a patch that looked like an ace. Two Aces meant you had flown two hundred missions. You would also have the squadron patch and your call sign patch. Dice games, and card games would be played. When other crews would spend the night at The Rose Garden they would be hosted at the Club. It was not unusual to have our FAC's come in for a night or two, or have Air America crews visit.

One night an Air Force Jolly Green Rescue chopper crew came in and the PJ (Parachute Jumper) shared this story with me. Seems the Jolly Green was over North Viet Nam when they began to pick up an aircrew's rescue beacon. They began asking the Air Force Air Controllers if all the birds were accounted for and they were assured that no birds were down. Still they had this Emergency beacon and they steered towards it until they were over the jungle where the beacon was transmitting. Was it real? Did the Viet Cong have a beacon? The pilot asked the PJ if he wanted to go down and check it out. Well, PJ's have a certain reputation and so he said yes, he would go check it out.

They slowly lowered him down on the penetrator and when he broke through the foliage he saw two American aircrew. However, they weren't Air Force aircrew they were Navy! One was badly injured and the other was OK. They lowered a stretcher and got the injured man into the Chopper and then the PJ and the other aircrew rode the penetrator up to safety. The Navy Pilot explained they had been hit hard. They had lost all electronics and most of the control of the aircraft and had just managed to get away from where they had been bombing before having to eject.

The Jolly Green pilot then said, "Why don't we take them out to their Aircraft Carrier?"

They began to ask the Air Force for permission but that was not going to be OK so they pretended they were losing their radio and proceeded out to the carrier anyway. Amazingly the air craft carrier gave them permission to land, although the Jolly Green Pilot had never landed on a carrier deck before. The landing on the Carrier was uneventful. Once down on the deck the PJ accompanied the injured air crewman down into the ship to the Doctor's Medical Bay. After sharing all he knew, the PJ went back up to the flight deck but now the Jolly Green was not in sight. He was told his chopper had been lowered on the elevator and they were to spend the night on board the ship.

That night they were the guest of the recovered pilot's Navy squadron and they celebrated and were toasted and patted on the back until the Ship's Captain came in and informed them that they would be having breakfast at 0600 the next morning in his Private Captain's Mess with him. When they were done with breakfast they went topside again to get back into their Jolly Green. To their great surprise they found all the Navy crewmen standing at attention in their Dress Whites, and as they walked by they were saluted and cheered.

They took off and returned to the Air Force Base in Thailand, where they discovered the Navy Admirals had taken it up the Chain Of Command to the Pentagon where Navy Admirals met with Air Force Generals and orders came back down the Chain of Command to the squadron Skipper. Therefore, when they landed their squadron Commanding Officer met them at their chopper and simply said,

"Great job...but don't ever do that again!"

Around Christmas time we were excited to learn that Bob Hope and his Christmas show were going to make a stop at The Rose Garden. This show marked Bob Hope's ninth Christmas tour in Viet Nam. Operation Linebacker was suspended for thirty six hours during the time Hope entertained in Viet Nam and other American bases including the Rose Garden. Accompanying Bob were Red Foxx, singer Lola Falana and about a dozen American beauties. The show was again very funny and it was great to see some beautiful American women trying to lift the spirits of the Marines. Bob Hope and Les Brown made these USO Christmas Tours for over fifty years bringing laughter and hope to American troops all over the world. God bless Bob Hope!

One time my RIO and I were given the mission to fly a Phantom from Da Nang over to a Subic Bay Naval Air Station in the Philippines where the Phantom could receive some heavy maintenance. It was a long flight over water through bad weather, but we make it OK. When we got to the station we checked into the BOQ and were told the aircraft that we would be returning to Da Nang would be ready in a few days. That gave us the opportunity to visit some silver markets and explore the night life in Olongapo.

Olongapo is a small town supporting the Cubic Bay Air Station and featured bars and girls of the night. Olongapo sported fancy jeeps with unbelievable decorations with every possible surface festooned with shiny, waving objects. It was extremely fun to watch those jeeps motor around the town. The bars featured pretty women that would have multiple American boyfriends. When a boyfriend walked into the bar the hostess would welcome him and seat him. Then if the man had a girlfriend she would come over and expect the man to buy her a drink and she would smile and flirt for a while. Then she would go back to her other boyfriend and expect him to buy her another drink and she would laugh and flirt with him. I have never seen anything like it before or since.

We also took a helicopter up to a city called Baguio where they had silver mining and a famous market featuring silver necklaces, earrings and other items of silver. The trip was fun and diverting. I bought beautiful ear rings and a necklace for Susan. Two days later we were flying the new aircraft back into Da Nang and soon we were back into the combat routine.

Another time my friend Watchdog was flying a mission with his RIO Brew. They were up North and doing a bombing run when they were hit by anti-aircraft fire just as they released their bombs. At that point they were probably diving at the ground at about five hundred knots. Suddenly the aircraft became uncontrollable. With no control over the aircraft Watchdog had no choice but to try to eject but the aircraft was now pulling lots of negative G's and pulling the face curtain became impossible. So the only option was to try to pull the lower ejection handle located down between his legs. Watchdog can only get one hand on the handle but managed to pull it. Immediately the aircraft canopy was blown off and the pancake charges lifted the seat out of the aircraft and the ejection seat rocket motor ignited.

Watchdog, watched his aircraft hit the deck in a fireball and he looked all around for Brew. He saw no chute. His chute swung only a couple of times but Watchdog was already on the radio providing target information to the FAC. He hit the ground and folded up his chute.

You must realize that you are never supposed to eject out of a Phantom at that speed. Watchdog happens to be about six foot two and all muscle and for some reason he didn't break his neck or lose an arm or leg. Most aircrew would not have survived the ejection. Now he was on the ground and he hears the Viet Cong guns that shot him down. He also hears and sees other American fighters starting to circle his position and make bombing run after bombing run. He could tell when the Air Force Phantoms were making runs also because he could hear their nose Gatling guns hammering the Viet Cong.

A Jolly Green began to talk to Watchdog, planning to try to come pick him up, but he told them it was too dangerous, and he was going to try to move away from the guns. He thought he was lucky that he ejected so low and that it was unlikely that any of the Viet Cong actually saw his chute open so they might not be looking for him. He spent the night evading and was picked up by a Jolly Green the next day. His RIO Brew was never found. I visited Brew at the Viet Nam Memorial too.

In late November I got leave and had a short break with Susan in Hawaii. It was unbelievable to suddenly be in a lovely setting with my beautiful wife surrounded by people just living their lives and having nice vacations. What a contrast it was as I knew my buddies were starting to build up for the Operation Linebacker bombing attacks on Hanoi. Susan and I had a great week in Maui and then in no time I was back at the Rose Garden.

Operation Linebacker was a joint mission involving Navy, Air Force and Marine aircraft targeting Hanoi in an attempt to try to force them back to the Peace Talks negotiating table. It was a huge undertaking with hundreds of aircraft participating. Some fighters were assigned MIG Cap which meant if MIGs were detected getting airborne the MIG Cap aircraft would be given directions to intercept and engage the MIGS. These were high profile missions with lots of publicity if a MIG was shot down, so only the Air Force and Navy got those MIG Cap missions.

Bar Caps were missions where fighters would be set as a barrier in case MIGs were trying to attack the bombing elements. Marines got to fly those missions. Operation Linebacker also featured hundreds of fighter bombers, B-52 bombers, Wild Weasels, etc. To take off and join an aircraft armada of over a hundred combat aircraft on one mission was awesome. As the flights got near Hanoi we could see the SA-2 supersonic, telephone sized missiles that were being fired at the B-52s far above us. It was exciting and dramatic to see the air power that America could bring to the battle. Advice: Don't mess with America!

Speaking of B-52's, it was always interesting when flying to hear an announcement over the radio that an Arc Light attack was happening at such and such coordinates in five minutes. Immediately the RIO would start studying his map trying to figure out where the bombing was to take place, while the pilot would be scanning the sky above looking for B-52 aircraft. On the ground you could easily see where B-52 bombing attacks had occurred as the ground looked like it had mini moon craters. You did not want to be the target for an Arc Light attack. Of course, the danger was if your aircraft happened to be UNDER the B-52s when they dropped their ordinance load, because they would destroy you in an instant if they hit you.

In February the Viet Nam war ended and I remember we had a huge "end of the war" party. We had a Thai Rock and Roll Band, and everyone was drinking and dancing with a rubber doll and just going absolutely crazy. The next day we got orders that our combat missions were going to continue, only now the targets would be in Laos. Laos missions were very dangerous. After a couple of months we had an "end of the war" party for the end of the Laos missions. The next day we were flying missions over Cambodia. They were not as dangerous as Laos, but the weather became a factor as we were flying long missions with a full five hundred pound bomb load, carefully picking our way through huge thunderstorms that featured awe-inspiring lightning and turbulence.

After about twelve months and one hundred and eighty combat missions I finally received my orders to go back home. During my last week the Aircrew hosted a going home party at the O' Club tent for me. A few words were said, and then they presented me with a special gift. It was a small copy of the Udorn's O' Club front door with a hole punched into one of the doors. Priceless. My last combat flight was May 2nd, 1973.

On the way home I spent two weeks in Japan buying stereo gear and cameras. After that it was flying back to Travis Air Force base in California. When we landed there, I actually kneeled down and kissed the ground. I had survived the war, and now I would get my reward. My next duty station would be El Toro Marine Air Base in Southern California.

Before that trip, I first got to fly up to Seattle, Washington and finally see Susan, my family, and my friends. Susan looked beautiful and she greeted me and reminded me of what I had been missing. It was terrific!! My family reunion was also warm and it felt good to be home. I also saw my old college friends who had written to me at the Rose Garden. I had changed, and they were into their new lives, and I realized that "the good old days" were now definitely in the past. We were all moving on.

CHAPTER EIGHT

FLEET'S TALES ONE

This chapter Contributed by Shadow's squadron mate, call sign—Fleet, while both were serving in The Rose Garden

Shadow was in the Red Devils squadron in the Rose Garden, I was in the sister Phantom squadron next door – The Silver Eagles. I was a RIO who joined the squadron while they were in the Rose Garden. After about four months of fairly intense combat flying out of the Rose Garden, I was deemed OK to take new pilots on their first combat hop. RIO's were in short supply and high demand, and we had to learn quickly.

One of my first hops after taking on this new role was to fly with a new guy I had just met and did not really know. He was a west coast trained pilot so I figured he must have it together pretty well. I also knew I had to have my act together because first combat hop could get weird quickly, and I knew because my own first combat flight had been very weird.

He seemed very attentive during the briefing and he asked a number of questions, which was to be expected. On the walk out to the Phantom he was quiet and seemed a little jittery, which was OK, because it meant he had his head in the game. I gave him the deluxe walk around tour and inspection of the aircraft. I pointed out pens, fuses, flags, and where they were stowed by the plane captains. The same had been done for me.

The mount up, start, taxi, and radio checks were normal. We were OK to do run ups and to take off and join up on our lead. Now airborne, we checked each of the aircraft to make sure all the bombs were still on board, the pins removed, and that we had no leaks. We proceeded to the Airborne tanker, and refueling went well with a first try stab and connection success.

From the Airborne Command and control, we got our vector and radio frequency for our Forward Air Controller (FAC) and the area were we to proceed to. Like most areas in Laos, it was considered to be hot and heavily defended. My pilot asked if I had been there before and I said, "Not exactly this target, but close." We drilled on and soon switched to our FAC's frequency. The FAC told us what our target was and the local altimeter setting. He shared what the terrain was like, what defensive fire we could expect, and finally, where the best bail out direction and area was if we were hit and then had to eject.

We spotted the FAC's aircraft and he marked the target. These were trucks at the bottom of a hill. He marked the target with a Willie Peter Phosphorus smoke rocket. Flight lead called that he had the target, and he was cleared in hot to drop his bombs. Lead's bombs were short of the target, and the FAC corrected and supplied us with an updated aiming point. He told us where to drop our bombs based on the smoke of Lead's bomb hits.

I asked the pilot if he was ready, and made him double check his switchology, altimeter setting, and the amount of fuel we had left. We were cleared in hot, and he pulled the nose around and dove toward the target. All was quiet as I read off the airspeed and dive angle. Everything was as it should be. I gave the stand-by call, and then the "Mark," at which the pilot was supposed to release the bombs. At the end of my Mark call I felt the nose come up, but it was too quick and too hard. This was not good. He pulled the nose up and swung around so we could see our hits. I twisted back to see the hits, and saw only dirt geysers and dust. We climbed back up to altitude and the FAC reported: "Two, you put bombs up the hill, down the other side and some into the next grid square. You slung them!"

I said to my pilot, "You gotta trust my Mark and settle down. The ground comes up fast at 500 knots. Settle down. My ass is in this bird too and I am not going to let us become a smoking hole. Shake It off. You can do this."

I heard him sigh over the intercom that showed he was listening and that was good.

Lead rolled in again and hit one truck. The FAC agreed that he had taken out a truck and a small supply dump.

We were clear and we rolled in again. Looking bad in the air in front of your buddies is the last thing a pilot wants to do. We rolled in with good airspeed and dive angle. I called stand by and then Mark. I felt the bombs kick off the aircraft after the right interval. I twisted around and saw blue smoke and white smoke. We had hit something.

The FAC reported,

"Better run Two! One truck destroyed and a stack of supplies hit. You saved your ass on that last run. Not bad..."

We rejoined with our lead and checked each other over again while heading back towards The Rose Garden. All the bombs were off, with no visible hits by their guns and no leaks of fuel or hydraulic fluid.

My pilot keyed his cockpit mic but said nothing. I told him he was on hot mic and we could debrief back on the ground. He said,

"Yeah, I fucked up."

I said, "No, you really didn't and it was better than my first combat hop," which was true, but that is another story.

Back on the ground during the post flight walk around, our plane captain showed us five enemy small arms holes in our aircraft that we had overlooked. My pilot was incredulous, and silent, and then he asked me if this happened on every hop.

I answered, "No, but it happens often enough!"

We walked to the maintenance shed and reported the aircraft as OK, but with five small bullet holes in the left outer wing panel.

Our plane captain came up and asked how he had done within earshot of the pilot.

I answered,

"Not bad for a new guy, not bad at all, but I bet he will listen to his RIO in the future."

I had the opportunity to fly several more hops with this pilot, and he became very good. He would always bring up that first hop we shared. I would always give him the same comment, that for a first hop he didn't do too badly.

After The Rose Garden I learned later that in 1980 he had transitioned into the AV8 Harrier B and had ended up flying into the water somewhere and had been killed. The AV8 Harrier was an aircraft with vertical take-off and landing capability, but not easy to fly. It was also a single seat aircraft with no back seat for a RIO. When I heard of his death, I was sad, and thought to myself— he might still be alive if he had an asshole RIO in his backseat.

PART THREE

Life at the Top

CHAPTER NINE

DEATH RATTLERS

When Susan and I arrived in El Toro, California in June of 1973, we found ourselves a nice three bedroom house in Mission Viejo, a growing community set among the Southern California orange trees. For the first time, we actually bought a house. Thirty three thousand dollars! I found a back way to the base driving my red Austin Healey 3000 sports car with the top down. I followed the road around the perimeter of the base until I came to three tall hangars. The middle hangar had a large rattlesnake painted on the side. The Death Rattlers logo looked good. I parked the car among the other hot cars parked by the hangar and climbed the long stairs up to the upper level where the admin offices and Ready Room were located. Along both walls were photos and plaques from the Death Rattler's history. I walked into the Ready Room and noticed a rattlesnake in a cage, and behind it was the flight schedule. I gawked at the sight. It had so many flights scheduled. I had never seen so many scheduled flights on a squadron schedule.

I heard someone behind me, and turned to see a Marine Major with RIO wings behind me. He introduced himself as the XO and welcomed me aboard and then said, "Let's go see Lancer."

The Skipper, Lancer, was well known. I had heard he had more F-4 time than anyone else, and that I would be lucky if I got into his squadron. Lancer was a little over six feet tall with a receding hairline but good looking, confident, and had a small grin. I was a confident, young Captain with close to two hundred combat missions under my belt, but I was still a little nervous.

He stood up and asked me a couple of questions about my time in Nam, and a little about my wife, and if we were all settled. Then he asked, "Captain Taylor, how much ACM have you flown?"

I answered truthfully, "Not much."

"That is what I figured, you having come to us from the Second MAW. Don't worry about it. In a couple of months you will be up to speed," he said.

"What's your call sign?" he asked.

"Shadow" I replied.

"Well Shadow, we fly clean F-4s. We fly more than any other squadron, and my job is to make this the best ACM squadron in the Marine Corps. Our troops do a great job keeping our aircraft in an Up status. We fly smart, we fly safe, and we will fight anybody, anyplace, anytime. Welcome aboard!" He finished and shook my hand.

BAM! I had checked into a dream squadron. I could fly almost as much as I wanted. I was going to fly clean F-4s with good weather almost every day against every kind of adversary aircraft. I only had one problem. I was an experienced combat pilot but with little ACM experience.

Quickly I met other pilots and RIOs. Red was another combat pilot from a sister squadron at the Rose Garden, and also Air

Force trained. OJ was the AMO. Stuff was a young pilot yet to go overseas, but with tremendous F-4 ACM experience already.

Dog was the Operations Officer and a former Viet Nam helicopter pilot that had earned a Navy Cross while in Nam. It seems a platoon had been hit pretty hard and needed to be pulled out. Two other choppers had tried and took so much fire they couldn't land and refused to return. Dog accepted the mission and although his chopper was taking heavy hits they managed to land, while continuing to take enemy fire, and pulled out the Marines and in doing so saved many Marines lives. A Navy Cross typically means you sacrificed yourself to save others and you should have been dead doing what you did, but somehow you survived. Dog was a real combat hero.

The Scheduling Officer came in to the Ready Room and I recognized that it was Jumper. He gave me a big smile welcomed me aboard and told me that Lancer had asked that he and Milo take me under their wing and brush me up on my ACM. He introduced me to Milo. Milo was about my height with a little mustache and a mischievous smile. He was probably one of the best ACM RIOs in the Marine Corps.

Lancer had laid out a simple goal. Fly more Air Combat Maneuvering than any other squadron in the Navy or Marine Corps and do it safely. I soon found out that the Snakes flew Phantoms clean with no external fuel tanks. The average flight would be forty five minutes to one hour and the goal was to turn out the best fighter pilots and RIOs in the Corps. You could feel the energy in the building. Maintenance would work twenty four hours a day so that when aircrew came down to fly, the aircraft were in the Up status and with good radars.

I discovered that pilots and RIOs would be fighting to get sorties in trying to get the most flights in a month. I was soon flying twenty five to forty missions a month. The majority of them were ACM. The Operations Department would call squadrons from all the other services and anywhere in the country to find squadrons that wanted to fight the Snakes. We had yellow business cards made with the Death Rattler Logo and a simple message: "Anyone - Any Time - Any Where" and the Snake phone number. Every weekend the Snakes would send out aircraft to fly and fight all weekend long. The only simple command was that they were required to be back by Sunday night with UP aircraft.

That meant that one weekend we might be deploying to Tyndall Air Force Base in Florida fighting Air Force F-106s, and another week we might be deploying to Navy Dallas to fight Marine Reserves flying F-8 Crusaders. We fought Navy F-14 Tomcats out of Miramar Naval base in San Diego and it was not unusual to fly against Top Gun classes and instructors flying F-5s and A-4s.

Unbeknown to Jumper, I had actually met him many years before when I was a student going to Washington State University. I was on the track team as a seldom used high jumper. WSU had an excellent high jumper who was jumping over six foot eleven. One weekend the University of Southern California came to Pullman for a track meet and with them came a high jumper who was one of the top jumpers in the nation. My job at that meet was to place the high jump bar on the standards as the jumpers cleared higher and higher heights. Finally I remember the USC Jumper had a very distinctive stride and he looked too heavy to be a high jumper. But striding up to the bar the USC jumper slammed his foot into the ground and soared over seven feet. That set a WSU field record.

I also remembered that when I had first checked into the Red Devils I saw a runner jogging. His run was a distinctive striding and I realized it was that USC high jumper from years before. I later discovered it was a pilot with a call sign of Jumper, but he was checking out of the Red Devils soon. I barely got to know him and then he was gone.

That began a focused course on learning to fly ACM. Day after day we would take about thirty minutes to brief. We would then go down to the locker room and put on our G-suits, our safety harness, and grab our helmets to then proceed out to the maintenance shack. We would be assigned a clean Phantom. We would walk out to the flight line and inspect our bird with our plane captain. I would climb up into the cockpit and the plane captain would follow me and strap my RIO and I into our ejection seats. A yellow cart with a jet engine would pull up and connect to the Phantom and I would begin to wind up our two J-79 Jet engines. We would check all the systems and salute the Plane Captain as my RIO got our clearance to taxi.

At that time I was reminded that it takes close to two hundred Marines in the Electric, Hydraulics, Radar, Avionics, Ordinance, Quality Assurance, and Ejection Seat Shops to make this flight happen. The salute by the plane captain proves that he and the maintenance team have invested their reputation and pride in the aircraft you are flying. Failure of the aircraft means the Shops have failed. Being the tip of the spear is what I had signed up for, but first you need a sharp spear!

We would generally do a section formation takeoff and then climb the aircraft out over the water west of San Clemente Island to engage in ACM. Sometimes Milo would fly with me and sometimes he would fly with Jumper.

When you engage in ACM you typically start nose-to-nose with about twenty miles of separation so you are out of visual range. Each RIO attempts to locate and lock on the adversary. When you are in good AIM -7 Sparrow missile range (about ten miles) and the radar dot was centered you would yell, "Fox 1!" In real combat a Sparrow would have been launched. Now you are likely in visual range and you need to see your adversary or you will soon be dead. Now the two aircraft close in on each other nose-to-nose. If you don't go nose-to-nose it gives the other aircraft space to begin maneuvering behind you. If each aircraft is going close to five hundred knots, you pass each other going a combined thousand plus knots. If you are really close the passing causes your canopy to shake and rattle.

As soon as you pass you begin looking over your shoulder, trying to keep your eyes on the other aircraft, all the while pulling four to six G's. Remember, when you pull five G's, it is five times gravity, so if your arm usually weighs ten pounds it now weighs fifty pounds. Your G-suit begins to inflate across your belly and lower legs attempting to keep the blood in the upper part of your body so you don't pass out. The oxygen system starts putting pressurized air into your oxygen mask so you can keep breathing. Talking becomes difficult. If you pull too many G's you begin to lose your vision first at the periphery and then your vision becomes smaller and smaller until your eyes are open but you can't see anything and you are close to passing out. If you pull too many G's the aircraft can be broken, which your maintenance crew and Skipper really don't like. For the Phantom, that number of G's was around seven.

However, if you don't pull enough G's, the adversary aircraft will pull inside your turn. But… pulling G's reduces your speed, and the less speed you have the less G's you can pull. If the Phantom gets slow you are dead (Speed is Life!) because you can't pull enough G's to stay effective. So one has to manage aircraft speed, G's, and of course fuel. You learned to be very judicious in the use of afterburner.

The goal is to maneuver your aircraft to arrive behind your adversary and in Aim-9 Sidewinder range, which is a little less than a mile within a small cone. When you arrive at that position you put your reticle on the adversary and your Sidewinder actually begins a winding growl noise; that is a wonderful sound to hear. At that point you would call, "Fox 2!" This is typically followed by a "Knock it off" call.

Different aircraft like different types of fights. For example, a Mig-21 and an A-4 like horizontal fights because they turn so well. The F-4 likes a vertical fight because it has so much power. In a vertical fight you are taking the nose up vertically then pulling down towards the other aircraft and gaining speed while you begin to pull G's. If you don't have a good shot you reduce the G's build up your speed and zoom back up to the top and hopefully into the sun so your adversary can't see you. Oftentimes when the fight was F-4 versus F-4, you got into weaving fights rolling around each other getting slower and slower. The noses keep getting higher. The airspeed dies. You begin flying using only the rudders. The RIO starts checking the altimeter to make sure you both are still above ten thousand feet. You may get so slow that you put your flaps out one half for a little more lift. You are looking down at the ground, then up at the sky, then straight ninety degrees down, and then ninety degrees straight up. You are right side up, and then upside down. You are pulling positive G's, and then negative G's, all the while looking at your adversary and listening to your RIO.

At the end of a fight, when it is knocked off, you are breathing deeply, sweating, and mentally reviewing what you did right and wrong. You are discussing the fight with your RIO. Then you head back to your twenty miles separation and start again. Flying against different aircraft required different tactics. Against the A-4 you had to fight a vertical fight, and drive the A-4 down to a slow speed until the A-4 finally had to drop the nose to pick up airspeed. That was the point where the F-4 could swoop down and get the kill. Fighting an F-106 was different because the F-106 could make one really impressive turn, but then it would be out of airspeed and could be beat.

Fighting the new-at-the-time F-14 was tough, because they had excellent radars and speed. Unfortunately for them they were huge, so you could see them at a distance and begin maneuvering early. They would start with the wing swept back but as they got slow their moveable wing would start moving open and forward, so you could accurately judge their airspeed. We flew against the first F-14 squadron, VF-120, and then started flying against the first two operational F-14 squadrons VF-1 and VF-2. Over time you began to know how to best fight every aircraft we fought. Every aircraft had advantages and weaknesses, and over time we learned how to minimize the Phantom weaknesses and take advantage of its strengths against the other aircraft's weaknesses.

When flying out of El Toro at the end of an ACM flight, we would often fly south and drop down in Miramar Navy Air Station in San Diego, where the Top Gun school was based. Miramar had a unique ground refueling set-up called the Octagon. It featured eight refueling stations around a circle so that eight aircraft could keep their engines running and hot refuel; and then taxi out with your wingman, get clearance, and then take off back into the Warning Area and fight again. The Snakes flew so many sorties out of Miramar that the Octagon crew thought we were stationed there. VF-1 and VF-2 valued VMFA-323 as adversaries so much that they made arrangements that whenever the Snakes refueled at Miramar using the Octagon, they would even pay for our jet fuel. Sweet.

During my ACM brush up, day after day we would follow this routine and at the end of each flight Jumper and Milo would debrief the flight and cover what I had done well or what needed more work. I kept getting closer. I also kept my head up because I knew I was fighting the best ACM pilot and RIO I knew. Finally we went out to the Warning Area and fought several times with no losses. We went down to Miramar, refueled, and then went back up and fought again. At the end of the day neither of us had scored a Fox 2. Jumper is one of the two or three most competitive pilots I know. He hates to lose or tie but above else, he is a professional and a team player. This time when we were back to the Ready Room to debrief, he shook my hand with a big smile, and Milo did the same with a little smirk. Lancer wandered into the Ready Room. Jumper went over and talked with him for a minute. Lancer walked over to me, looked me in the eye and with a big smile said, "Nice Job Shadow. Now you can begin training our new Snakes!"

While flying with the Snakes we had the opportunity to upgrade our equipment and aircraft. The Marines had developed and wanted to test some new technology. We received special helmets molded specifically to our heads featuring a new Visual Target Acquisition System (VTAS). The helmets would be fitted with a small (one inch) glass reticle that was attached to the helmet and that you could look through. The idea was that when the RIO locked up an adversary aircraft on his radar, you could look through the reticle. When the adversary aircraft subsequently came within your visual range, he would be spotted within the VTAS and you could then potentially yell "Fox 1" and fire your AIM 7. You would then begin maneuvering early for a potential AIM-9 Sidewinder shot. Whenever you were in range, besides the Sidewinder growling, the VTAS reticle would begin to blink, and you would call Fox 2. This technology really worked great and allowed us to particularly see smaller adversaries earlier, because if we could radar lock them, then we could see them when within range. The key was having a good radar and a talented RIO. Another nice feature was that I got a brand new helmet painted the way I desired; with SHADOW printed above the visor.

Before I go on, I also need to explain that although Jumper and I focused on flying one versus one in the beginning, the more important engagements were multiple aircraft versus multiple aircraft. For example, in a two versus two engagement you and your wingman go into the fight with a specific strategy;

where one aircraft may go straight by the lead aircraft as close as possible while the wingman is sweeping up or slicing down, hopefully unseen, to shoot the lead bogey aircraft soon after the pass. Over time the Snakes perfected a tactic called The Hook VID. With this tactic the first aircraft that got a radar lock up became Lead. The wingman would then aggressively make a rapid vertical separation from the lead aircraft. Now the lead aircraft was flying nose to nose with the bogey. Ten to twelve thousand feet below him or above him would be his wingman. The wingram was watching his lead visually while his RIO was trying to find any other aircraft. As the lead aircraft came close to passing the bogey, the wingman would be watching the bogey passing his lead and be already aggressively pulling his nose straight up (or straight down). As soon as the bogey aircraft passed our Lead, the wingman would already be rolling in on his six o'clock and be calling Fox-2. This tactic invented by a Marine aviator with a call sign of Hook was extremely effective and very difficult to counter. Also with our VTAS systems, the Hook VID became even more effective, and we would always be looking to shoot AIM-7 sparrow missiles early in the engagement.

Now imagine entering a fight with four versus four or more aircraft. Suddenly everything changes. You have to assume that no matter what you are doing, someone is targeting you and beginning to maneuver to shoot you. If you are closing in on a bogey's six o'clock to shoot an Aim-9 Sidewinder, you better know where the bogey's wingman is, or he may be shooting you. In larger engagements everywhere you look you see an aircraft, so you need to quickly go through a list of assessments.

The first thing you try to establish is whether the aircraft you see is friend or foe. If it is a bogey, then you need to quickly assess who has the vertical advantage. The higher you are the better, because you can trade your altitude for speed. Who has the better turn radius? If the bogey has a superior turn radius you better not get in a turning engagement, so you stay fast and vertical. Which aircraft has superior speed at any point in the fight? Fast is good, slow is death.

Finally, you ask a simple, but difficult without experience, risk/reward question. Should we engage with that aircraft with the potential quick reward of a kill? Can we get that shot without getting killed ourselves? The potential reward is balanced against determining how great the risk appears, and the decision has to be made instantly. The more bogey aircraft, the greater the reward and risk. At the same time, you always have a wingman, and your primary job is to keep your wingman safe. These engagements proved another crucial value of the RIO. The pilot is engaged and focused on flying, and looking for the kill. At the same time, the RIO is constantly scanning the sky around the aircraft, and particularly checking our six o'clock and our wingman's six. He is noting altitude and airspeed, and asking fuel status, knowing that the pilot is committed to the fight; so he becomes the safety valve.

So you are checking your altitude, airspeed, and fuel state. You are talking and listening on the radio to other aircraft in the fight and communicating with your RIO. You are pulling G's and making instant decisions on risk versus reward. In the F-4 Phantom one thing was always true: **Speed Is Life!** If you got the least bit slow in a multi-plane engagement, you became a stationary target for everyone in the area to see and shoot; and even your ability to bug out and leave the fight would be severely compromised. Although you would always try to enter a fight with a tactic like the Hook VID, after the fight started it would quickly break down into a giant fur ball, with aircraft potentially close in sight, and others out five or six miles. Some bogies could be below you and some above you. That is when you needed a strong RIO, a great wingman, and the discipline to stay fast and fly vertical.

It's funny, but after flying so many flights and fights in the Phantom, it began to feel like just an extension of your body. You could make it do whatever you wanted. You knew what it could and couldn't do. It was strong, powerful and safe if you treated it with the respect it deserved. Air Combat Maneuvering takes every bit of concentration, stamina, adaptability, situational awareness, and aggression that a person can muster. After an ACM engagement I was both worn out and exhilarated. It was a HIGH.

I now joined Jumper, Lancer, Stuff, OJ and others taking the new guys up and teaching them ACM. One thing that always impressed me was that the older, experienced RIOs would have to fly with the new guys. Bombing runs, night intercepts, bad weather formations, and ACM. Going straight up and straight down while pulling too many G's (or not enough G's) with a pilot that was just learning how to fly the Phantom. RIOs are crazy and fearless. In the Snakes we had Milo, Ski, and Spider who were top RIOs. We had RIOs with big personalities like Obie, Smoky, and Cowboy that made the Ready Room and bar sizzle.

During this time with the Snakes we were blessed with extremely talented pilots and RIOs. Some young pilots like Casino, Slim, Grunt, and Buzz were just naturally good sticks. Others had extensive experience, but in other aircraft. For example, Crazy had thousands of hours in crop dusters and would just love the opportunity to fly his aircraft slow with you. Each had their own personalities and eccentricities. Most had hot cars. Casino and Slim had fast corvettes. Grunt had a Ferrari Dino that would turn heads wherever it went. Snake had two Jaguar XKE's. Of course there were exceptions. Dog had a Volkswagen Thing, and Jumper always had nothing cars, as he preferred to put his money into real estate.

All aircrew were smart, confident, in good shape and extremely competitive. Occasionally a pilot or RIO would join the squadron that lacked something. It could be not enough aggression, or too much aggression with a lack of good judgement. It could be spatial awareness or trouble with instrument flying. They could be bad at bombing or be failures at working the radar. Whatever, they would not last long in any squadron, and particularly the Death Rattlers. We had Naval Academy graduates, Air Force Academy graduates, General's sons, former Marine grunts, helicopter pilots, and even former Blue Angels. If you were good, you could fly with the Snakes.

Many aircrew were married and the wives and girlfriends tended to be young, very attractive, confident, and smart. The Snakes had squadron parties that were memorable. I should also mention that on Friday night you were expected to go to the O' Club and hang out with the Snakes. There were dice games and drinking games. You could lose a dice game and suddenly be buying drinks for twenty Snakes laughing and swapping lies. Some pilots and RIOs had O' Club Bar acts that had helped establish their reputations just like the flying. Imagine a bar in Southern California full of young, tan, sweaty, flyers in their green flight suits, drinking, boasting, toasting, laughing, flirting with pretty wives and girlfriends and enjoying life. That is what Friday night at the O' Club was like in the 70's. Often times I would be talking with Jumper or Casino and we would just laugh and say, "Can you believe we get paid to do this? We would do this for free!"

While at El Toro I was sent to Aircraft Safety School. This school was located up in Monterey, California. The area was beautiful and the weather was perfect. I would attend class every day until three and then go out to the base golf course and practice my golf. At Safety School I learned how to become a squadron safety officer. The job was to keep the squadron focused on eliminating incidents and accidents. If an accident did occur then the Safety Officer's job was to help lead the accident investigation. When an accident happened, then typically the squadron XO would lead a team of investigators. We would examine the accident site, look through pilot and RIO flying logs, research aircraft maintenance logs, and interview anyone associated with the crew or the maintenance. It was a difficult but important job as we needed to know not only why and how the accident happened, but what could be done to prevent another accident. It was not unusual for aviators to die and for Skippers and AMOs to lose their squadrons when accidents occurred, so it was a very serious business.

Of course, not everything was perfect. One time we lost a young pilot and RIO when during an ACM engagement they had accelerated in afterburner right into the Pacific Ocean; while looking over their shoulder running away from an adversary.

Another time, I was inside the hangar and I heard a tremendous roar and whooshing sound. Anybody in the area knew that sound and knew that an ejection seat had just fired. I ran outside and saw that one of our aircraft was just stopped in the taxiway. There was a body lying beside the aircraft. I ran over and immediately discovered it was our AMO. It turned out that they were taxiing in after a flight, and he was unstrapping from his ejection seat. When he raised his seat, something apparently caught on the ejection seat rocket motor… and he was ejected through the canopy while in the ejection seat but not strapped in. He died on the flight line while I was leaning over him.

Another time a TA-4 was coming in for a landing and the cockpit started clouding up so bad that the pilot could not see outside the cockpit. The pilot and RIO thought the aircraft must be on fire. Both aircrew ejected and floated down in their parachutes. Unfortunately, when they ejected the TA-4 lifted its nose back into the air and began flying again—**with no pilots**! Word spread like crazy and soon everyone on the base was standing outside the buildings as the aircraft circled El Toro. Sometimes the aircraft would dive, and other times it would climb, but always circling the base. Every person was making their own mental plan of what they would do if the aircraft started diving down in their direction. Finally, the aircraft nosed over and crashed beside the end of the runway hurting nobody, and destroying nothing. Whew.

Of course, learning to handle failures of different items in the aircraft was a part of becoming an experienced aircrew. For example, if you were flying and had a utility hydraulic failure, it would mean that you would have to blow the landing gear down using compressed air. Because of the loss of hydraulics, your brakes were seriously compromised, so an arrested landing using the landing hook was the solution. The aircraft also had PC1 and PC2 hydraulic systems, but if you lost those, you were likely to eject. The loss of an engine was not surprisingly serious, but depending on when you lost it determined just how serious. For example, if you were just taking off and had a full fuel load and maybe external tanks or bombs it was extremely serious. If you had burnt a lot of your fuel and were returning to base, then the Phantom had enough power in the remaining single engine to enable you to make a safe landing. The loss of oxygen systems, electrical systems, and experiencing various smaller component failures were handled almost routinely. The ability to handle aircraft issues and judge the relative risk was an important part of the maturing experience.

Lancer was the Skipper for my first year with the Snakes, and it was an awesome year. The Death Rattlers flew more hours than any other Navy or Marine fighter squadron—by a significant amount. The squadron under Lancer had no aircraft accidents or incidents. By the time Lancer left the Snakes, the squadron had built tremendous momentum and discipline, so we continued to excel; but it was not as much fun.

Just because I was now a Captain with lots of hours and experience did not mean I could and would not do stupid things. Once, while on a cross country with Slim piloting the other aircraft, I proved that fact. We had deployed to Navy Dallas on a cross country and spent the night. In the morning we were going to return to El Toro. We went into the planning room and pulled out a map and plotted a course to fly to and land at Sheppard Air Force Base at Wichita Springs, Texas. We taxied out and took off. We were flying contentedly along and discussing various topics when Slim called on the Radio and inquired where we were going. My RIO and I start looking closely and realize we had been navigating to Wichita, Kansas not Wichita Falls, Texas. Suddenly we were in trouble because of our location and fuel state. We quickly calculated that our best and almost only option was to climb and aim for Albuquerque, New Mexico. We immediately did that, and then began carefully monitoring fuel and distance. As we approached Albuquerque, we found ourselves having to penetrate a cloud cover, and learned that the air field had a very low cloud ceiling and some ice on the runway. Perfect. Now we had to fly the approach as a section, split up when under the clouds and on short final, and then land separately. Our fuel was now extremely low so we could ill afford to do a Go Around. We broke out of the clouds, separated, and landed safely. We taxied in and looked at the fuel gauges. Extremely low. Whew! Stupid! ... and, I was supposed to be the one teaching the younger guys.

During my second year the Snakes were informed that a special Project was being initiated. It was called "Have Idea". It was a project to test the F-4 Phantom tactics against special adversaries. We were informed that three aircrew from each squadron in the Navy and Marine Corps would compete against special adversary pilots flying F-5 and A-4s. The winners would get to participate in Have Idea representing the F-4 flying community.

The pilots for the Snakes were Jumper, Casino and myself. The RIO's were Milo, Ski and Spider. We started intensive ACM flying sessions working as a team and individually. Of course it helped that we could fly more sorties than any other squadron because our maintenance was so good. Meanwhile the squadron worked on getting our Phantoms as perfect as they could make them.

We started to fly against different adversaries and we did really well gradually reducing the competition until there were just two squadrons – The Snakes and one final Navy F-4 squadron. When the competition was over we were chosen as one of the two squadrons to compete in the project. At that point we were flown to Nellis Air Force Base near Las Vegas where we were put into a room and given a brief on this special project called Have Idea. But hold on... before the briefing we had a Secret Service Agent walk into the room. He informed us that what we were going to be told was considered Ultra Secret and that if we told anyone what the project was about, including our wives, we would be sent to Leavenworth prison. OK, this must have been pretty serious stuff, because we all had Top Secret clearances even before coming to the briefing. By the way, this project remained Ultra Secret for decades and was only declassified after the turn of the century. That is why I can write about this now.

Once we had signed our lives away, we were informed that the United States had two MIG-21 Fighter Jets and one MIG -17 Fighter Jet procured by who knows what means. The MIG-21 and MIG-17 were the front line Russian/Chinese fighters that the Viet Cong and Chinese had flown in the Viet Nam War. "Have Idea" was to pit us against VX-4 pilots out of Pt. Magu Naval Base and Top Gun Instructors from Miramar flying the MIG's. All the aircraft would carry modern telemetry equipment and tracking pods so that every engagement and missile shot could be tracked and studied.

The following week we flew four Phantoms into Nellis AFB along with a small maintenance team. The maintenance team was not told what the mission was, but they knew it was something big because only the best personnel were selected and suddenly whatever aircraft parts they needed were made immediately available.

The flights would be conducted over the Top Secret Area-51 Range. They could only be conducted at specific times when it was known that no satellites were over Nevada. I was always hoping when flying over Area 51 to maybe see a UFO, but no luck.

The plan was for Jumper and Milo, and Ski and I, to fly two Phantoms against two MIG -21s. Casino and Spider would fly one versus one against a single MIG -21. When we were successful on a Fox 2, that MIG would be informed they had to immediately leave the fight. If one of the Snakes were shot down, we had to leave the fight.

We flew six missions against the MIG's, two versus two. Ski and Milo were phenomenal at picking up the MIGs out over the desert quickly, using the Pulse Doppler radar. We would then go into our Hook VID tactical attack that we had planned for that mission. Using our VTAS system we would try to get a visual on both bogey aircraft as early as possible. Hopefully we would both be shooting Aim-7 sparrows before Lead would pass one of the MIGs. Meanwhile, the wingman would be maneuvering out of the Hook VID to get a quick Fox -2 on the first bogey, while the lead aircraft and both RIOs were making sure the other MIG was not a danger to either of the Phantoms. After one MIG was knocked out of the fight, we would both team up to fly a vertical fight, keeping our speed up and making slashing attacks and gradually bleed the remaining MIG's airspeed down until one of us could nail him with a Sidewinder.

After seven days and multiple fights we had been successful, and had won more than our share of fights against serious adversary aircraft and superior, experienced pilots. This proved that the tactics being taught by Top Gun to Phantom crews, if flown correctly, could be successful. Of course we did not win every engagement and so I had the opportunity, when losing, to make a couple of observations. First, the small MIG -21 was very difficult to see and without a radar lock they would sneak up on us easily. Second, if you got a little slow, the MIG-21 could turn like a bandit and be inside your turn and having guns on you astonishingly quick. It reinforced the Phantom dictum "Speed is Life!"

Casino also did extremely well flying one versus one against the MIG-21. He and Spider flew a vertical fight using VTAS to shoot the MIG-21 with Sparrows to begin every fight, and then flew a smart strategy when into the fight. At each pass, if the MIG started turning port (left) then Casino, rather than turning port with the MIG, would instead turn starboard (right). This was called the opposite circle fight. This would create additional distance between the aircraft and thereby provide another opportunity to fire a VTAS head on AIM -7. This also avoided getting into a slow speed turning fight, which the Phantom would typically lose against a MIG-21. Casino again proved the value of speed, VTAS, and the Phantom's ability to fight vertical fights against the MIG.

We flew down to Miramar after the project was completed and had a debriefing in front of the Navy and Marine aviators and brass. When we were introduced the Top Gun lead said, "Listen up! These guys know what they are doing and had more success than anyone else in the Have Idea Project." That was nice to hear!

When we flew back into El Toro and turned into the flight line, the entire Death Rattlers squadron greeted us. They did not know any details, but they had been informed that the Snakes, for the moment, ruled the fighter world. That was a highlight moment in my flying career. However, it was also strange, as we were not able to talk about it for decades.

The two years with VMFA-323 were two of the best years of my life. Susan and I were going to have a baby. We lived in beautiful Southern California, and I drove a little red sports car. I had the opportunity to fly almost daily, and to train with the best. I got to serve and observe inspirational leaders. Personally for me, "Have Idea" validated my confidence that I could fly the Phantom with anybody. It also provided me the opportunity to choose my next assignment. There was one Top Gun opening, so Jumper chose that opportunity and became a Top Gun Instructor. Casino still had to serve an overseas tour, which he did. I chose the opportunity to have an exchange tour with the U.S. Air Force stationed in Fort Walton Beach, Florida. Susan and I sold our nice house and moved again. This time we were heading east, and going to the pan handle of Florida.

CHAPTER TEN

LANCER

It is indeed fortunate if, at some point in a person's life, they are exposed to an inspirational leader. In my case, I had the opportunity to serve under such a person twice. This person was Lancer. When I knew him, he was always called either Lancer (his call sign), Skipper, (as squadron Commanding Officer) or Colonel Mike.

When I first met Lancer he already had a distinguished career. He had joined the Marine Corps and finished flight school in 1956. He had served two combat tours in Viet Nam flying F-4 Phantoms with over four hundred combat missions. He had served an exchange tour with the Royal Air Force and served two tours as the F-4/F-8 Flight Test Officer at MCAS Cherry Point, North Carolina and North Island, California. He had over 5,000 hours in the F-4 and I personally didn't know any pilot who had more hours than Lancer did.

His experience automatically meant you never questioned the wisdom he shared with those of us who got to know him. The first thing you learned to appreciate about Col. Mike was that he loved to fly, and that he was good. Some squadron Commanders did not share that love of flying and they were not always strong pilots. Lancer especially liked Air Combat Maneuvering.

But Lancer was not just an aircrew leader. He loved aircraft maintenance, and he appreciated the dedication and focus it took for our maintenance teams to keep our Phantoms not only flying, but flying safely. You could find Col. Mike wandering around the maintenance area at 0500 in the morning and he would probably still be there at midnight. He talked and laughed with the maintenance troops. He knew their names and where they came from. He knew if the wife was having a baby or if a car had broken down. He knew who was good and who was exceptional. He also loved the Marine Corps, and although we were as aggressive as any squadron could be, it was always expected that we would not embarrass the Corps.

When I joined the Snakes the average Marine Corps and Navy F-4 squadrons were flying between two hundred and three hundred and fifty hours per month. That meant the average aviator would be flying eight to fifteen hours a month. Maybe twenty five percent of those hours would be dedicated to ACM, and most squadrons flew the F-4 with centerline tanks.

Lancer had a different view towards what he thought an aircrew needed. His view was simple. Develop the best ACM pilots in America by flying more ACM than anyone. Fly ACM in clean (no centerline) Phantoms, and fly against every adversary he could find. Yes, you needed to know how to fly intercepts and drop bombs, but the Snakes goal was to be the best at ACM! After all, if you wanted to be King Kong in the fighter community, you had to shoot down five enemy aircraft and thereby become an ACE. You could only become an ACE by winning at ACM.

When you engage with a true enemy aircraft, the first thing you do is blow off your external fuel tanks so that your aircraft has its maximum performance capability. For that reason, Lancer believed that the Snakes should fight the Phantom clean with no external fuel tanks. Unfortunately that meant that where other squadrons were flying missions that logged 1.3 flight hours, the

Snakes would be logging ACM missions with about .8 flight hours. Unless we flew more sorties than other squadrons, the Snakes would have less flight hours. It is important to know that a squadron Commanding Officer's performance was largely measured by the number of monthly flight hours the squadron flew. So Lancer was taking a risk, and banking on his maintenance team.

Also, if you were potentially going to eventually fly ACM against enemy aircraft from anywhere in the world, an F-4 aircrew had better practice and gain experience flying against different types of aircraft with different strengths and weaknesses. If you wanted to be the best you would have to challenge and beat the best, so part of the Snakes' mission was to compete against Marine Air Warfare Tactical Units as well as pilots from the Navy Top Gun School.

When you joined VMFA-323 you were quickly indoctrinated with the notion that you were joining a squadron that would lead America in ACM quantity and quality. That didn't just mean aircrew. It meant that every maintenance Marine, every Logistic Marine, and every Admin Marine would buy into the mission. Every Marine that joined the Death Rattlers would be introduced to Colonel Mike, and he would share his vision and then tell them how they could personally contribute.

After I joined the squadron I watched the hours begin to grow from three hundred to four hundred. Then from four hundred to five hundred and from five hundred to six hundred. The Snakes were out flying every squadron in the Navy and Marine Corps. At every squadron gathering we celebrated our progress and success and outlined our next target. Every aircrew, maintenance chief, plane captain, or maintenance technician knew what we were doing and took immense pride in our success. In fact, Lancer set out a special incentive. If the Snakes hit their hourly goal for the month all the troops would get a day off. That was very popular. In addition, if the squadron flew every aircraft in the inventory on a single day he would buy and bring the maintenance team a couple cases of beer.

Almost every week on the Snake flight line, aircraft from around the country would be parked. One week it might be F-106 Air Force Delta Dart fighters from Florida. The next week might feature Marine Reserve F-8 Crusaders from Dallas. We fought F-104 Starfighters, Marine A-4 Sky Hawks, and AV-8 Harriers. It was not unusual to see Navy F-14 Tomcats or Top Gun F-5E Tigers. When deployed, every Aircrew carried Death Rattler Business Cards. The Yellow card had the VMFA-323 Death Rattler Logo and the invitation to fight Anyone, Anytime, Anywhere.

Over time, an aircrew learned how to fight the Phantom against the various types of aircraft. We learned you did not fight the F-106 the same way you fought the F-14. We learned Air Force Tactics, Navy Tactics, Israeli Tactics, and how to combat each.

Every weekend the pilots and RIOs would push and argue about who would get to take the Phantoms on cross country flights. This involved flying and fighting against each other or aircraft from different services around the country. Friday and Saturday would be spent at the BOQ at some foreign Air Base, with the expectation you would bring the Phantom back in one piece on Sunday in time for Maintenance to get the aircraft ready for Monday's flight schedule.

To maintain this level of flying, Maintenance had to be running hard twenty-four hours a day. No matter what time you visited the maintenance hangar it would be likely that Lancer would be down talking and interacting with the Marines. Laughing, sharing stories and telling them what a fabulous job they were doing.

The Snakes became an attractive target for new air crew members to want to join, and a target for other squadrons to disparage. But, gradually the two sister squadrons at El Toro, the VMFA-314 Black Knights and VMFA-531 Grey Ghosts, began to emulate the Death Rattlers. They also had very talented pilots and RIOs. Soon the Third Marine Air Wing became known as the ACM center of the Marine fighter community and the fighter hours the 3rd MAW was flying kept setting higher standards.

Part of the maintenance success of the Snakes was Lancer's relationship with the Supply and Rework facility at North Island. If we became desperate for an aircraft part Col. Mike would make a phone call to one of his old friends and the squadron would send someone down in a car to North Island and swap something for the needed part. For that reason our supply logistics were tough to beat.

One month Lancer had Operations and Scheduling set up a week long squadron deployment to Yuma MCAS in Yuma, Arizona. Yuma is where the F-4 Training squadron was located, but it was also surrounded by several Warning Areas that could be used for both bombing and ACM flight training. The squadron would take ten aircraft to Yuma. After getting settled it was announced that the next day the squadron would attempt to set a new record for F-4 sorties in a single day.

The plan was to fly fifty sorties before sunset. This would require every aircraft and aircrew to fly multiple times. If most of the aircraft did not stay in the UP status, the mission would fail. The flights were to be flights of eight aircraft with some of the aircraft carrying practice bombs and some carrying practice missiles. Adversary aircraft were also scheduled to harass the flights and provide ACM adversaries.

The first flight launched a little after dawn, led by Lancer. They returned and all aircraft were UP. Jumper led the next flight and again all eight aircraft returned in UP status. This continued three more times so that the squadron had flown forty sorties. The last flight was increased to all ten aircraft. At around 1700 the final ten ship flight launched and one hour later all ten aircraft landed and taxied back to the line and shut down. All ten aircraft were still UP!

What sticks in my mind is the fact that when the ten aircraft were shut down, they could all have been flown again. It was the most impressive feat of flying and maintenance that I have ever witnessed. The entire squadron met the aircraft and it was a celebration. Lancer was beaming and thanking and congratulating every maintenance and aircrew he saw. His vision, his challenge, his achievement, his record, and yet I never heard him take credit for that day. He only talked about what a great job everyone else had done.

Under Col. Mike's Leadership the Death Rattlers won the Pete Ross Award for Aviation Safety and the Robert M. Hanson Award as the finest Marine Fighter/Attack squadron in the Marine Corps. In 1974 Lancer was awarded the Alfred A. Cunningham Award as the Marine Aviator of the Year for his leadership of the Snakes. During Lancer's command, the Snakes had the highest reenlistment rate in the Marine Corps.

By the way, I served with Lancer later in my career when flying with a Reserve Phantom squadron, the VMFA-112 Cowboys out of Dallas, Texas. It was my luck to be squadron Commander of the Cowboys when Col. Mike was the Group CO. His house was right by the maintenance hangar, so once again he hung around the maintenance teams constantly. Again the Cowboys won the Robert M. Hanson Award as they were out flying every Marine squadron regular or reserve. Eventually Lancer was to become a Major General. This is one of the few times a true operational leader was promoted to this level.

After serving with Lancer not once, but twice, I can offer five characteristics that I personally observed that I believe served him well. I believe that, if followed, these five characteristics would lead to exceptional leadership and rewarding success anywhere:

1. Share a passion and vision for what you want the team to achieve.

2. Challenge your team to achieve extremely difficult but ultimately highly rewarding goals.

3. Make the striving fun.

4. Personally welcome and involve everyone on the team.

5. Celebrate and recognize team and individual contributions, but claim no credit for yourself.

I am grateful for making the acquaintance of this inspirational leader who made an indelible impression on me as a young Marine. Later I often found myself reflecting on this list, and I can only smile as I made many choices thinking, "What would Lancer do?"

PART FOUR

Flying with the Air Force

CHAPTER ELEVEN

THE GOLDEN PRIDE

In May of 1975 Susan and I arrived in the Florida Panhandle, at beautiful Ft. Walton Beach. We immediately found a nice house in Shalimar, Florida and started to make it our home. The big difference was that Susan was now pregnant with our first child, so we now had to make a baby's first room and buy all the required books and baby stuff.

Meanwhile, I checked into Eglin AFB and the 59th Tactical Fighter squadron, officially The Golden Pride, but known as the Lions. The Lions were flying the F-4 E Phantom. This F-4 E Phantom was different in several significant ways. First the aircraft featured slats. Slats are small surfaces on the leading edge of the wing. The slats would extend during slow speed maneuvering and create more lift. This meant that at slow speeds, you could still use the stick and ailerons to fly and not have to switch to using only the rudders. Second, the F-4 E had a 20 MM Gatling Machine Gun (the M61A1 Vulcan) located underneath the radar in the nose of the aircraft. It had also featured an Inertial Navigation System (INS) that provided superior navigation and performance bombing. Finally, it did not have a refueling probe. More about that later.

When I arrived, the Lions had a Marine Corps aviator that was leaving the squadron soon. He introduced himself and then introduced me to others in the squadron as he began bringing me up to speed on what I could expect to encounter in an Air Force fighter squadron. Once again I was the new guy and the outsider. However, I felt that with my combat experience and recent time with the Snakes, I would be able to fit in and perhaps help them in ACM.

Unfortunately, the Air Force believed in flying with two wing tanks at all times and they absolutely considered it a mistake to fly the F-4 into a slow speed fight. I agreed with the principle of not getting into slow speed fights. However, I tried to make the point that in combat the pilots would be blowing off their wing tanks and at some point they might get slow, unintentionally, when being attacked by multiple adversaries. Therefore, I thought it would be wise to practice flying from time to time, without wing tanks, and also learn to fight slow just in case. The Air Force disagreed. So I found that when engaged in ACM I could normally win fairly easily. When I became a Flight Lead, after a scheduled mission, I would try to teach the pilots that wanted to learn how to fly the F-4 E effectively in ACM.

However, the Air Force had a different set of priorities. They worked on things that were strategically and tactically important, but sometimes new to me.

The Lions divided the squadron into four Flights. A, B, C, and D. Each flight had a Flight Leader Pilot and Weapons Systems Officer (WSO). In the F-4 E the WSO had a stick and throttle, but limited instruments and poor forward visibility. The WSO's basic job was much like the RIO. It was to use the radar to find adversary aircraft, work the INS to navigate, and perform other tasks in sophisticated bombing modes.

I started off in one of the flights as a pilot but quickly worked my way up to be a two ship formation lead, and then became a four ship formation lead. Eventually, I was given one of the four squadron Flights to lead.

The Air Force took bombing very seriously. Again, we typically dropped small practice bombs, but we also got to fire the nose gun. Soon one of my responsibilities was to become a Range Officer. That called for me to drive a jeep way out into a forest until I came to the bombing and gunnery ranges. At the range they had a tower that looked like a forest ranger's tower. In that tower you would have a radio and binoculars. The job was to watch the aircraft drop their bombs and score their accuracy while also acting as the Range Safety Officer (RSO).

Just like the Marine Corps, the Air Force bombing patterns were basically ten degree, thirty degree, and forty five degree bombing. The aircraft would circle the target, calculate the wind effects, and then roll into releasing the bombs at between four hundred and five hundred knots. That was interesting to watch, but what I loved was the gunnery range. At the gunnery range the F-4 would accelerate to about four hundred knots and fly a shallow, ten degree pattern and then aim and fire at a white target about the size of a bed sheet. The Air Force had a system that would count the number of rounds that hit the target, which I would relay to them by radio.

If you are anywhere in the vicinity, the sound of an F-4 Phantom going four hundred knots is very loud. Already fun! Now fire a twenty Millimeter Cannon capable of three hundred rounds per minute in slow fire, or six hundred rounds per minute in fast fire. That calculates to five to ten rounds per second being fired out of an aircraft already going four hundred knots. That aircraft speed combined with the 3,450 feet per second muzzle velocity of the M61 Vulcan produced 2,800 mph bullets. Watching the bullets impact the ground leading up to and through the target, at a speed you could not comprehend, was simply mesmerizing. No dodging those bullets. You would hear these five inch long bullets going supersonic and it wouldn't sound like a gun. It would sound like a high powered mechanical buzz saw. I loved it.

Another duty was to sit in a small shack at the end of the runway and make sure a landing aircraft had its wheels down and locked before landing. I thought this was a stupid waste of time. Another duty was to go up into the Airport Control Tower. In that capacity you were responsible for all the squadron airborne aircraft, and you would make all the necessary calls and decisions in case of accidents, emergencies or bad weather. That was both interesting and educational, and sometimes I felt I helped avoid an incident or accident. I enjoyed being up in the tower.

Fort Walton Beach was a great area to live. It had beautiful white sandy beaches, inland waterways, and enough night life to make it interesting. Many of the aircrew had boats that could pull water skiers and so that was a favorite weekend activity. Susan and I did not have a boat, but others always liked guests to join them on their boat, so we were often on boats.

After about four months at Eglin, Susan and I had been blessed with a baby boy we named Ty. We had practiced Lamaze birthing techniques and everything went according to plan. Susan's post pregnancy was going well until suddenly a hurricane (Eloise) became a potential threat to the area. Unfortunately, that meant the aircrew would have to fly the aircraft out of the hurricane path and into a safe area. In our case it meant that I had to say goodbye to Susan and our brand new three month old baby boy, and fly one of the Phantoms to Texas for the week. Meanwhile Susan had to pack up and take Ty to a secure building on the base until the hurricane passed. By the time I came back, Susan was back in the house and we then had to address the damage that had been done. Susan and the other wives did not appreciate their husbands abandoning them in the face of a hurricane. I had to agree.

During my time with the Lions we had some outstanding deployments. One took us to Alaska, and another to Hawaii. We also deployed to Nellis Air Force Base, in Nevada for one of the first "Exercise Red Flag" (still going today), and I even ferried a Phantom to the Shah of Iran.

The deployment to Alaska called for us to fly from Eglin AFB in Florida to Anchorage, Alaska. It was more than a ten hour flight, and since we were flying over Canada and Alaska in the middle of winter we had to wear heavy winter flight suits in case we had to eject. I have to tell you—the thought of ejecting at three hundred fifty knots and drifting down at freezing altitudes just to land in the middle of a forest, in Canada, and in the snow, was not a pretty thought. We had to refuel multiple times because of the length of the flight.

Aerial refueling in the Air Force was very different from the Marine Corps. The Air Force used KC-135 Stratotankers, which were cargo jets redesigned to refuel jets. They flew at around thirty one thousand feet altitude, and at a little over three hundred knots. That meant the aircraft that were taking on fuel did not have to slow down, and in fact could fly formation with the tanker and just move over and refuel when fuel was needed. The KC-135 had a long boom which had a hose with little wings so that the operator could essentially fly the boom. The operator sat in the back of the KC-135 and could see the fighters clearly as they came up to refuel.

The Air Force F-4 E had no refueling probe. Instead, there was a refueling port, just behind the WSO's canopy on the top of the F-4. The F-4 pilot would maneuver the F-4 using guide lights on the bottom of the KC-135. Once in position the boom operator would fly the refueling hose into the refueling port and commence refueling. The F-4 pilot's job was to just maintain airspeed and keep the aircraft level and within the guide light parameters. The Boom operator was responsible for completing the refuel. I felt this manner of refueling was superior in two ways: first, the refueling took place at an airspeed (over three hundred knots) that was comfortable for the F-4 pilot. Second, the refueling at high altitude was better for maintaining a safe altitude and not wasting fuel trying to slow down and descend to meet a C-130. The downside of the Air Force aerial refueling was that you were totally dependent on the skill of the boom operator, rather than depending on your own developed refueling skills.

I remember one strange thing that occurred when we were about half way through the flight to Alaska. Our flight received a radio call from our XO informing him that his wife had just successfully delivered a bouncing baby boy. I expected some hooting and hollering or some kind of expression of happiness. Instead the Colonel responded with a simple, "Roger!" He was on the Air Force fast track to become a General and was always pretty serious, but I thought that was taking it a little too far.

Ten hours in a small fighter jet cockpit while sitting on a hard ejection seat was not fun, and I became anxious to hurry up and land at Anchorage. However, as we approached Anchorage we were informed that the Air Field was closed to landing traffic because the field had zero visibility.

That meant that we would now have to divert to our back up landing base, which was King Salmon, Alaska. That was another two hours to the West. Two hours later we arrived over King Salmon, only to find its weather was also degrading. Unfortunately, now we had no choice, because we were too low on fuel to divert to anywhere else. I was a two ship section lead within a four ship so we broke up into two flights while above the clouds. We then made an instrument approach down to King Salmon. When we finally broke out of the clouds, the landscape looked like the surface of the moon, with endless small craters. We made a formation landing, taxied in, and shut the engines down. We staggered out of the aircraft and were laughing, happy to just be safely on the ground.

Because King Salmon was not expecting to have twenty aircrew spending the night, we were split up and put in different housing quarters. My WSO, Gazelle, and I were assigned to the Alert Hot Pad hangar. We were to go upstairs and grab a bed in one of the bunk beds where the alert crews were sleeping. Down below us in the hanger there were two F-4 Es standing Alert on the Hot Pad. We said “Hi" to the crews, dropped our flight gear, and flopped into our bunks.

Two hours later we heard an alarm siren, and suddenly the Hot Pad aircrew were jumping out of bed and putting on their flight gear. Unfortunately, in the confusion, the Alert pilot was putting on MY gear. I told him he was putting on the wrong gear. He stopped and then sleepily starts putting it on again. I told him again that it is my gear he is putting on. He finally got it and put on his own gear and slid down a fire pole to where his F-4 was waiting. One F-4 engine was already started when the aircrew clamored in and started the second engine. A couple of minutes later, we heard them taxi out of the hangar and heard the afterburners light as they took off into the night.

About one hour later the aircrew came back up to the bunks. They told us that they had intercepted a Russian Bear Bomber (Tupolev Tu-95) that was flying near the U.S. border. The American and Soviet pilots waved to each other, and then the Russian Bear turned back towards Russia while the F-4s headed back to King Salmon.

In the morning we discovered that the King Salmon Base had every building on the base connected by tunnel, so that a person never had to go outside into the winter weather. Neat! The next day we flew our Phantoms back to Anchorage and the weather was clear. However, the runway and taxiways had ice. Landing and taxiing the aircraft was OK, but we found out that you couldn't precisely park the aircraft where you intended. Instead, the aircraft just kept sliding. We just aimed the aircraft where we wanted to park and slowed it to as slow as we could. We then shut the engines down and the aircraft stopped wherever it stopped. The ground crew would then hook the aircraft up to tow tractors and park them precisely.

Another better deployment was taking the entire squadron to Barber's Point Airfield on Oahu, Hawaii for thirty days. For those thirty days we would wake up and maybe fly one bombing mission over a special Hawaiian Island reserved for bombing. If no flights were scheduled, we would go surfing or visit the waterfalls or just lay around the pool. The one really memorable flight was a day when we were scheduled to fly over to the Big Island and support an army ground unit. We flew over to the island and flew the briefed mission and then when completed we heard the magic words from the ground platoon leader.

"Would you guys mind making a low pass over our troops?"

"Roger, that!" I responded while smiling. A green light to show off!

The platoon was spread out climbing up the side of one of the hills near the volcano. We flew out over the water and lined up with the hill. We accelerated until we had two Phantoms going over five hundred knots and extremely low so that at the end we were actually climbing the same hill the platoon was climbing. As we reached the platoon we plugged in the afterburners and pulled the aircraft straight up into the sky. The platoon leader called us and was laughing and shouting and told us we had actually blown a couple of guys back down the hill. They absolutely loved it and couldn't thank us enough. Grunts love an air show and a demonstration of friendly air power. We then flew over to the volcano on the Big Island and went down into the crater, did a lap, and then headed back to Barber's Point.

After a terrific month, we flew back across the Pacific Ocean and into California. That flight utilized a single tanker KC-135 dedicated to just my four ship formation. First Class!

A really demanding and memorable mission of a lifetime was when the Lions were tasked with delivering seven new F-4 E Phantoms to the Shah of Iran's Air Force. The basic mission called for the flight to originate in South Carolina, and fly the great circle route over the North Atlantic Ocean to Spain. Once there, we were to refuel and fly from Spain to Iran. Simple!

First we were taken to Seymour Johnson Air Force Base in South Carolina, where we were assigned our new Phantoms. We then had an extensive brief, and then the seven Phantom took off and rendezvoused with a tanker and another lead aircraft. That lead aircraft would be our primary navigator across the Atlantic.

The great circle route means you minimize time over the Atlantic Ocean, but you fly a more Northern flight path. The first part of the mission went as planned. My WSO, Drummer, and I talked about everything while refueling and navigating. When flying over an ocean you have plenty of time to think about what happens if something goes wrong and you have to eject. If everything works perfectly during the ejection, you will be floating down in a parachute thousands of feet until you land in the ocean. Then you have to ditch your parachute and make sure your flotation device works. Hopefully you then have a tiny raft that has inflated so you can climb into it and assess your new situation. You are a tiny speck, thousands of miles away from land and who knows how far away from shipping paths. You have a radio, a locator beacon, a mirror and a small amount of snacks. OK enough about that.

So halfway across the North Atlantic, when trying to refuel, my wingman, Deadbeat, calls to report he has had a hydraulic failure and can no longer take on fuel. We did not have enough fuel to continue to Spain nor to England so we only had one option; and that was to leave the rest of the flight and divert down south to the Azores. The Azores is a small island chain in the middle of the Atlantic Ocean, but fortunately they did have an Air Force Base. In both cockpits we were now pulling out various plates, maps, and calculating distances and potential fuel states. We were pulling out the approach information plates for the air field and determining what we were going to be facing when we arrived. The Azores runway turned out to have only one runway long enough for an F-4 to land. The runway was eight thousand feet long. Eight thousand feet is considered a short runway but would typically be OK. There were mountains on both sides of the runway, so we would just be making a straight in landing with maybe enough fuel to do one go around, if required. However, with heavy clouds and mountains on both sides, we knew that might be tricky.

The first problem was that in order to land on an eight thousand foot runway, the drag chute should be deployed to slow the aircraft down. Unfortunately, the airfield was calling for a direct crosswind to the runway. That was trouble. When the drag chute was deployed, the chute would be pulled by the wind in one direction, while the nose of the aircraft would go the opposite direction. Normally this is not a problem, because you have nose wheel steering to correct the steering problem and keep you on the runway. Unfortunately nose wheel steering is hydraulic, and Deadbeat has no hydraulics, so the plan had to change. The plan became: put out the drag chute and as soon as it begins to slow the aircraft, jettison the chute before it would cause the aircraft to veer off the runway.

We were flying in close formation in heavy clouds. We decided that as soon as we break out of the clouds, I would speed up and my aircraft would land first. That, of course, means I would be landing fast on a short runway with my wingman close behind me. He would be jettisoning his drag chute, so I couldn't use my drag chute or he might run over me.

Sheesh! Of course, any radio conversation among military or commercial pilots is required to be calm, potentially with dry humor, but in no case with any sign of panic or concern. We made our plan, and as we broke out of the clouds I saw the airfield on the nose and so began to accelerate as Deadbeat began to slow. Drummer watched Deadbeat and told me when the distance was sufficient. I immediately pulled the throttles back and we came in for a hot landing. The Phantom typically lands around one hundred thirty six knots. I was over that and quickly the air field yardage markers, that tell you how much distance you have until the end of the runway, began flying by. Seven thousand, six thousand, five thousand, four thousand and quickly three thousand. I then started breaking, and breaking hard. I watched as the end of the field rushed at us and I managed to get slow enough to take a turn off onto a taxiway at high speed, all while continually looking back to see what was happening with Deadbeat's Phantom.

His aircraft was obscured in a cloud of dust but I didn't see any ejection seats or chutes so that was good. When the dust finally settled, we could see the aircraft was off the runway sitting perpendicular to the runway but leaning to one side. Of course, the Azores Emergency vehicles were surrounding the Phantom, but we could see their canopies opening and we didn't see any fires, so that was also good. We sat for a minute to let the brakes cool then taxied into the parking area and shut down the engines. When we got out of the aircraft, Drummer and I just looked at each other, shook our heads, and grinned. A jeep came pulling up and an Air Force Officer got out. He introduced himself as the Base Doctor and then proceeded to pull out a bottle of scotch with a shot glass for each of us. He poured each of us a shot and then proposed a toast: "Nicely done, and welcome to the Azores!"

When all was said and done, Deadbeat's Phantom was broken and would take a while to fix. Deadbeat figured he had left the drag chute out a tad too long, and when the nose pulled over, he couldn't quite control it. Therefore, the aircraft skidded and a landing strut collapsed, but because they had wing tanks installed, the aircraft stayed upright.

We hung around the Azores for a couple of days and then Drummer and I received our orders. We were to take off the next morning and rendezvous with a KC-135 and continue the flight to Saragossa Spain on our own.

We got up the next morning and put our bags in the small baggage tank. The baggage tank is a small hollow tank that is attached to the Phantom where you might typically carry bombs. What happened next is one of the mysteries of the universe.

We said goodbye and taxied out to the end of the runway. Because jet fighters with afterburners were seldom seen, a crowd had formed to watch the takeoff. We taxied onto the runway and were cleared for takeoff. I put it in afterburner and we launched down the runway. As we lifted off the runway I kept the aircraft low while lifting the landing gear and flaps. With the airfield still in sight, and for no reason that I can explain, except... perhaps I was young, cocky, a show off, and a fool, I decided to do an aileron roll.

As you know by now, an aileron roll is typically simple, but I had never done an aileron roll while the centerline tank and wing tanks were full of fuel. Also, I was not at a high speed. I pulled the nose up and confidently started the maneuver. Drummer inquired if we were Ok, because he did know we were going to do a roll. I don't think he thought it was a bright idea, but he was silent. He just wanted to know if we had an aircraft problem and were maybe out of control. I said we were good as the aircraft continued its slow roll and I began to realize that I had made, potentially, a fatal error in judgement, as the Phantom was feeling very sluggish. I realized we were on the edge of stalling! If we stalled, we would not have the altitude to recover or successfully eject. I lit the burners again and after a couple of seconds our airspeed began climbing and we began to lift up and out towards our refueling rendezvous.

There was silence in the cockpit until Drummer remarked,

"Well that was interesting. Do you think we still have our baggage tank aboard?"

I looked at our G gauge and noted we had exceeded four G's recovering from the roll. The baggage tank was only stressed to remain aboard up to four G's. We rendezvoused with the tanker and continued on to Saragossa, without further incident, while wondering two things: Did we still have our baggage tank? Did anybody at the Azores Base turn us in for our unusual maneuver? The answers were: Yes, we still had our baggage tank and no, we had not been turned in. Whew! Boy, I am lucky.

The next morning Drummer and I went thru another long briefing for the mission to deliver the remaining six phantoms to Iran. The flight involved refueling a couple of times and flying through a narrow corridor, where if we got off course, we could be shot down. Drummer and I were tired after arriving late and not getting much sleep. We would be number three in the formation, so we didn't worry or pay strict attention to the brief. After all, we were number three, not the lead. We got suited up and started our aircraft. Shortly after starting, we heard the lead aircraft call that his airplane had an engine problem and they would have to abort. Dash Two said he had the lead and we began to taxi. As we approached the engine warm up area, Dash Two called and reported that his Inertial Navigation System would not synchronize and they would also have to abort. "Dash Three you now have the Lead," we heard.

Drummer responded, "Roger that, Dash Three has the lead."

Seriously? Drummer and I realized we were now the lead aircraft in this four ship going from Spain to Iran, featuring multiple refueling encounters, bad weather and a dangerous corridor to traverse. Drummer and I are now fully awake and pulling out charts, checklists, radio frequencies and flight plans as we took off over the Mediterranean. I can tell you the refueling went well. The weather was crappy until we got over Iran, so that the flight had to stay in tight formation for hours. We made it through the tight corridor, without getting shot down, and broke out of the clouds when we started descending over Iran into Tehran. When we landed, the Iranian Air Force teams swarmed over the aircraft to take possession and we were now simply Americans trying to get back to America.

The drive from the Air Base to the center of the city was perhaps the most dangerous thing we had done in the last week. The drivers had too much testosterone, and traffic lights and lane lines meant absolutely nothing. Our hotel was nice, but for the very first time as an American overseas, I felt disrespected and unwelcome. We were lucky to catch a commercial flight out the next day.

Not too long after that adventure, the Shah of Iran fell from power. I was told later that one of the Iranian Pilots that had trained with us at Craig Air Force Base had been made an Air force General under the Shah, but after the Shah fell, he was dragged through the street and beheaded. He was a very aggressive but likable young man, and represented his country well. It was hard to hear of his execution. He was the first of my Air Force Class to die.

Imagine a mock aerial war including adversary aircraft, air-to-ground bombs, ground-to-air missiles, tracking radars, and over one hundred aircraft in the air at one time. Add to that the notion that every aircraft is carrying a telemetry pod so that a ground computer can capture and track every aircraft, their speed, and altitude. This same range can report bombing accuracy, air-to-air missile firing accuracy, and effectiveness of aircraft radar and missile avoidance technology and evasive maneuvers. That range and capability exists, and the Air Force named the exercise to utilize them, Red Flag.

Every squadron in the Air Force participates in Exercise Red Flag sooner or later, and the Lions were no exception. We flew into Nellis Air Force Base in Las Vegas, Nevada and spent a week flying in Red Flag. For that week the entire squadron planned and flew complex air-to-ground and air-to-air mock combat scenarios. Each night the squadron would receive the mission and targets for the next day. For example, we might be tasked with flying into a heavily defended area and take out a known enemy radar site. The Lions would then be paired with other squadrons and different types of aircraft and capabilities and be tasked with putting together a detailed tactical plan that included map routes, communications, specific timing for attacks, attack directions, and back up plans.

On a single Red Flag mission you might be airborne with twenty-five other aircraft coordinated with your squadron. You might first perform aerial refueling and then drop down to a low level ingress route. We might attack from one direction or we might put specific times for different flights to attack from different directions. We might plan on using deception, including feints to lure adversary aircraft away from the primary attack force. After refueling, we would drop down to five hundred feet and five hundred knots following a carefully planned route using the map and our Inertial Navigation Systems. If we were being tracked by enemy ground radars, our RHAWS (Radar Homing And Warning System) gear would alert us with the direction and level of threat, and we would attempt to evade. If attacked by adversary aircraft, we would attempt to engage and defeat the adversary while our attack groups continued the mission. Sometimes we used standard ordinance and occasionally we utilized laser guided glide bombs. After hitting the target, the flights would have to try to successfully egress from the target without getting shot down. The missions were exciting, realistic, challenging, and important lessons were learned.

Once the mission was complete, the flyers would go into a special debriefing room that had large television screens that would enable the squadron to watch the entire mission. We would determine target success, aircraft losses and wins, and other important lessons, primarily because of the telemetry pods that were being carried.

Red Flag was awesome. It was challenging and realistic, where tactics could be created, tested, and evaluated in real time. It brought the entire squadron together as a unit because we were competing not just with ourselves to be successful, but also competing with the other squadrons. It was also fun to meet and engage socially with the aircrew from the other squadrons and aircraft.

At the end of my Air Force tour I had spent two years with the Golden Pride and the Air Force. Like with every squadron, I grew to love and respect the guys in the squadron. They were just as smart, cocky, well trained, and professional as well as fun loving and crazy as the Navy and Marine crews. They enjoyed drinking, partying and flying. Susan and I enjoyed the squadron's camaraderie and came to know and enjoy the Air Force traditions.

The Air Force has a promotion system that identifies Officers that are likely high level leaders, and puts them on a fast track. The aircraft are superbly maintained and the aircraft are not flown unless they are totally in an UP status. The various squadrons' performances were similar and predictable. Every squadron is likely good but not exceptional. If you are in command, you know what you are going to get. If the Air Force doesn't tell you that you CAN do something, then you can't do it.

The Navy and Marine Corps have a different approach that says if they don't tell you specifically not to do something, well... then you can do it. The Navy and Marine aircraft are flown with more aircraft issues. As a result, the aircrews typically have more experience handling aircraft issues. Over time this breeds a confidence and experience that allows them to handle anything that is thrown at them. The Navy/Marine Squadrons have more disparity between them, with some squadrons being below average and some being truly exceptional.

I loved the F-4 E Phantom. The INS, the slats, and the 20mm nose cannon made the aircraft fun and extremely capable. I would have loved to have flown an Air Force Phantom clean and fought some ACM. That did not happen.

With my Air force tour complete my next assignment was to proceed to Yuma Marine Corps Air Station in Yuma, Arizona. I was going to be tasked with teaching new pilots how to fly the F-4 Phantom. Susan, Ty and I packed our belongings and headed for Yuma. That, by the way, would be our eighth family housing move and the sixth state we had lived in during our eight years of marriage up to that point.

PART FIVE
Transition

CHAPTER TWELVE

SHARPSHOOTERS

Now we were back in the Marine Corps. We arrived in Yuma, Arizona and bought a house and again moved all our things from Florida into our new house. Yuma is a small town in the middle of the desert close to the Mexican border. It gets unbelievably hot during the summer. I checked into my new squadron, the VMFAT-101 Sharpshooters. This was a training squadron with the mission to train new aircrew how to fly the Phantom.

The squadron instructors were all very experienced and talented. The Ops O was a good pilot and very funny. I soon became friends with Rookie, Knute, T-Bone and Dump. The flying was definitely different. During the week I would be teaching academic classes about the F-4 and flying with the new pilots. On the weekends a few of the Instructor pilots and RIOs would try to head off on cross countries and have some fun.

I found being an instructor pilot challenging. It was not the flying, but instead the academics. For instance, I learned that I had naturally learned how to bomb. But now I had to teach a class and go into detail on how to fly a bombing pattern. I needed to teach how being fast or slow would impact bomb impacts. I needed to talk about the impact that wind might have on a bomb. Talk about different types of ordnance. I actually had to learn the details of what I had always done a little more by feel.

The same problems existed in Air-to-Air. Certain things I had learned just came naturally, but now my instructions had to clearly explain the steps needed to manipulate the stick and rudders needed to produce a specific outcome.

All the pilots were coming out of Pensacola Naval Training and if they had been selected to fly the Phantom then they were likely top students. Still, the Phantom was an intimidating beast. They were not familiar with the power and speed of the F-4. Afterburners were new as were the drag chutes. So everything was new: how to taxi, how to do engine run-ups, afterburner takeoffs, the secrets to aerial refueling in the Phantom, how to drop bombs, how to read the radar while flying, and how to accomplish formation take offs. Everything was new.

One time I was flying with a new pilot, and he was really struggling. You could tell he was really uncomfortable flying the Phantom slow with the nose very high and speed dwindling. That of course, made me nervous too, because that was one of the tricky parts about flying the Phantom without slats. This was when you had to transition to flying with just the rudders. Twice I felt him start to move the stick and felt the Phantom starting to stall and move the opposite direction. Right then my admiration for what RIOs endured was increased ten-fold. He also scared me in the bombing runs as he would roll in OK but end up too steep and release too late, meaning we were going too fast and coming too close to the ground before he would over G the aircraft to pull out. Finally he had trouble landing the aircraft. Three times I had him do go arounds because we were not aligned, or too slow, or too fast. His situational awareness was just not good.

I finally went to my Ops O, Mac, and asked him to fly with this pilot and tell me what he thought. He did, and he shared my misgivings, and so unfortunately we washed him out of the Phantom program. He was highly disappointed, which I perfectly understood, but I also felt that maybe we had saved both his life and a RIOs life by getting him out of an aircraft he simply could not handle.

I remember one time Knute and I flew on a cross country up to Hill Air force Base in Utah. There we had set up some flights with Air Force F-16s out over the Salt Lake warning areas. We were in a two versus two fight and I was pulling into a position at the six of the F-16 when my RIO, Dump, yelled, "Break down port now!"

Now experienced RIOs never yell, as they were trained to be calm and cool on the radio, so I jerked the stick left and down as quick as I could and felt my canopy rattle as Knute's aircraft flashed by just barely above me and in the space we would have occupied without Dumps call. I saw Knute's RIO, T-Bone, looking at us as they slid by and his eyes looked huge. We had missed a collision with each of us converging to a bogey's six but from opposite directions so our bellies were facing each other. How Dump saw him I'll never know. It was the closest I ever came to an inflight collision and it almost happened with my own wingman. Later when I was with the Cowboys I learned, that if you had talented and experienced pilots fighting, they would both be trying to get to the same place at a bogey's six, and the chance of an air to air collision was actually higher with your squadron mates than with other bogey aircraft.

Yuma, Arizona is a hot desert. During the summer it can get to one hundred and fifteen degrees. That makes pre-flight and taxiing the Phantom miserable, because the air conditioning in the F-4 does not function until you are flying. It also meant our outdoor runs that we would do, which were typically three to five miles, were very challenging. Rookie and I would be jogging and talking about anything to keep our minds off the heat. I remember running one day and somehow we were talking about something and suddenly Rookie was trying to calculate the volume inside some container as we were running. What? Some of these guys were pretty bright.

The desert was also beautiful. One night we took a bunch of four wheel drive vehicles out into the desert and had a big bonfire. Seeing the desert during the day we realized it was actually beautiful. At night, out in the middle, away from all the lights except the campfire, it was spectacular, particularly the stars. That night one of the boys had a little too much to drink, and as we followed the road back out of the desert in a small caravan we saw him parallel to us, out maybe one hundred yards. He was going very fast and as he hit each dune or cactus patch his truck lights would go high into the air and then look like he was going to dive. We could also hear his engine and listened as he flew up into the air and then crashed back down. We watched him until he was out of sight, and we wondered if he was wearing a crash helmet. When we got to the main road we saw him sitting at the first gas station with his hood up; and radiator steam pouring out of his engine. You can't fix stupid.

Another fun incident happened when they were filming the third Star Wars movie out on the desert near Yuma. We were eating at a bar and restaurant and found the Star Wars crew were hanging out at that same bar that night. We started to talk with them, including Princess Leia (she had a wicked sense of humor). We told them what we did and they asked us to do a fly over the next day at around noon. They would clear it with the Director. We talked to our Ops O and the next day we made a four aircraft, low altitude, high speed pass over the Star Wars set where Luke Skywalker was going to walk the plank. We ran into them a couple nights later and they said they loved it but they cut our scene from the movie I guess.

It was 1978, and I had now been in the Marines for over 10 years and had had spent all my time in squadrons. That was unusual, as Officers would typically end up going to some school or non-flying Group or Wing duty. So although I was lucky to still be in a squadron flying, I knew my squadron time was coming to an end. Soon I would be assigned to Group staff or Wing Staff. I might be sent to one of several senior officer schools. I had another plan. I would leave the Marine Corps Regulars and join the Marine Corps Reserve. They were starting to fly Phantoms and I knew several of them from my VMFA-323 days flying against them in their F-8s. I also wanted to try to join an airline and start a new career while continuing to fly fighters in the Reserves. That was my plan.

I finally made my decision, informed my Skipper, and then he had me go talk with the Commanding General. The next week I had my last flight. It was very emotional when I made my last flight with the Sharpshooters. As I taxied in to the line I realized that if I was unsuccessful getting into the Reserves, this would be my last time in the Phantom. After ten years, I might be done. I was sad and a little scared but I got out of the Phantom, patted it on the nose, and walked away.

CHAPTER THIRTEEN

THE BRANIFF INTERLUDE

As emotional as my final flight in the Phantom was and leaving the Marine Corps, I realized I need to let that go and move forward confidently to solidify my future. First order of business would be to get into the Marine Corps Reserves. Second then to be hired by a commercial airline and enjoy the time off and the money as I heard so many pilots relate. All of this while having the fun of flying F-4s with the Reserves. It was the perfect plan and the perfect dream.

The first step was to get hired by Continental Airlines and join the VMFA-112 Dallas Cowboys Marine Corps Reserve squadron. The Cowboys had flown against the Snakes many times, back when I was with VMFA-323. The Cowboys were flying F-8 Crusaders then, and were very experienced fighter pilots, so we had enjoyed close fought battles in the air and became friends at the bar in the evenings. Now the Cowboys were transitioning into the F-4 Phantom. When I decided to leave the active Marines and try to fly with an Airline and join the Cowboys I had a sponsor that helped with both. He greased the skids for me to join Continental Airlines, and soon I had passed the tests and interviews and only had to get a rubber stamp physical check to join Continental.

Susan and Ty waited in the car while I went in to take my physical, anticipating a big celebration that evening when we would learn where I might be stationed. After all, I was a Marine pilot in excellent physical condition and I had never failed a physical in my life. However, I was stunned to suddenly find myself sitting on an exam table in front of the Doctor who was telling me that he felt my Glucose scores were the precursor to me becoming a diabetic; and so he could not allow me to join Continental. I remember feeling clammy all over, and suddenly sweating, and although the Doctor was standing in front of me speaking, all I could see was his mouth moving and could not hear anything. I was in shock! I was thinking about how I had voluntarily left the Marine Corps and now I had no job, no home, and no plan, and my wife and child were sitting out in the car, waiting for the good news.

So the first part of my plan failed when the Continental Flight Surgeon said I was not qualified to fly with them because he felt I was a risk to become a diabetic (forty two years later he is still wrong). The second part of my plan was also delayed, as the Marine Corps Reserve Phantom squadron in Dallas (VMFA-112) was not adding pilots at that time. This was not good. My plan was falling apart right in front of my eyes, and I did not have a good back up plan.

Wow, the first thing I could think of to do was to apply for a job with a fabulously successful Real Estate Agent that we had worked with in the past. She agreed to take me on and teach me the real estate business, but after two weeks I realized that I just had to pursue the Airline pilot job until I was sure it would not work.

Susan and I agreed that she, her mother, and Ty would move up to Washington and live free in a small, primitive cabin owned by my folks. In the meantime, I would need to get a Turbojet Flight Rating in the Boeing 727 and an Air Transport Pilot License if I wanted to improve my chances of getting hired by a commercial airline. Both would require attending specific schools.

The first school I attended was training in order to earn a Boeing 727 Flight Engineer Turbo Jet License. That school was being held in Santa Monica, California located by a small airport in May of 1978. The first day there I met the other three students in my class. All were former military pilots. One was a Navy P-3 pilot, and the other two were an Air Force B-52 bomber pilot, and a C-141 cargo pilot. For the next few weeks we were immersed in learning about the Boeing 727. We learned the electronics, the avionics, the hydraulics, fuel systems, flight controls, instrument gauges, circuit breakers, etc. It was very intense, with a test after each section. We basically went to class during the day and studied during the evenings. We were spending a lot of money to attend and our future commercial airline success required this step to be taken so we were serious.

After a few weeks of academics we started flying a 727 simulator. The simulator was located in Burbank, California. The only times we could fly the simulator was from 2:30 to 6:30 in the morning. That meant we would drive over to Burbank at about 1:30, and then one of us would fly the simulator while the other three took naps until our turn. The simulator was basically a reproduction of a Boeing 727 cockpit. You had a Captains seat on the left, a First Officers seat on the right, and sitting perpendicular and behind the First Officers seat was the Flight Engineer's seat and his panel. The instructor sat outside the cockpit but he could set the aircraft to take off out of any airport in the world. The instructors not only taught us how to fly but also how to work the Flight Engineer panel. In addition, they just buried us with simulated emergencies. I can tell you that trying to fly the simulator at three AM in the morning was not ideal.

One night on a weekend, a woman one of the students knew, invited us over to her house for drinks. We got there and the friends started to pull out some Marijuana and asked us if we wanted to join them. I had never tried Marijuana and I knew that some of the airlines in their interviewing process would have the pilots take a lie detector test. One of the questions they were supposedly asking was, "Have you ever done drugs."

So I said, "No." I would take a pass as did two other students. However, the fourth student joined them and had a good time. Unfortunately for him, when he did get an airline interview they did conduct a lie detector test, and he failed and was not hired.

Our final part of the training was to drive to Phoenix, Arizona where the school had rented a Boing 727 for the evening. Each of us was to have the opportunity to take off, fly and land the Boing 727 at night.

I had not flown an aircraft in months, and had never flown a large multi engine aircraft featuring a yoke and three engines. When it was my turn, I crawled into the pilot's seat and realized how foreign this felt despite having flown the simulator. I taxied this monster out using the nose gear steering and lined up for takeoff. When we were cleared for takeoff I advanced the three throttles and we started down the runway. It felt much slower than the F-4 (no afterburners) but also fast, because I had not flown in a while and it was night time. We hit take off speed and I pulled back on the yoke and we were airborne. I remembered to call for the gear and flaps to be raised and we flew around a little and then came back into the pattern for a landing.

It felt very strange and different. Flying a fighter aircraft required the Phantom to be able to respond to small flight control movements quickly. So for example, the Phantom would roll with just a little motion of the stick. However, large commercial or military aircraft required stability and gentle turns because you were either carrying cargo or passengers. Therefore, the Boeing 727 seemed to move very slowly to me, and it took a full turn of the yoke to make a banked turn. Also the engines would take a little time to spool up and give me the thrust I wanted. Nevertheless, we finally arrived at a final landing approach. I was keeping the wings pretty level and we were on the glide slope, but I realized that I really did not have any of the visual clues as to when to raise the nose so that we could make a smooth landing. All I knew was that we would have to raise the nose a lot sooner than we did with the F-4. My instructor pilot told me to start easing the nose up and bam, we were on the ground and rolling out. Now I had to remember to pull the thrust reversers up to slow the aircraft before I started braking. We stopped and I taxied the aircraft to where the next student could take his turn. Whew, I found out I had passed and now I possessed a Boeing 727 Turbojet Certificate.

The next day my three companions and I started our drive to Dallas, Texas. I was scheduled to attend an Air Transport Pilot (ATP) Training course the following week. I rented an apartment with an Air Force friend of mine and soon he and I were in ATP school. This school was taught at Love Field in Dallas. It focused on teaching you all the things you needed to know to be a commercial Airline Pilot regarding navigation, fuel rules, approaches, etc. The flying consisted of learning how to fly a small Citation jet that featured a very modern cockpit technology such as you would find in commercial airlines. Again the school was challenging with academic tests and a flight test, but after a few weeks I had successfully passed and received my ATP in June of 1978.

Now I just needed a commercial airline interview. My two best hopes were Braniff Airlines and Southwest Airlines, both headquartered in Dallas. At the same time, I was continuing to stay in contact with the Cowboys hoping for an interview with them. While waiting for them I got a job as a security guard that called for me to watch a big building and area and take hourly walks around and punch time clocks to show I had checked the areas. I used the time to work on what I hoped would be a persuasive airline interview final statement. I also worked on preparing for the different tests I knew the airlines used to reduce pilot candidates.

When I finally got my interview, I received one from both Braniff and Southwest at about the same time. After the interview and testing I received offers from both. Yea, at last!

So I had to make a choice. Let's see... Braniff was the fastest growing airline in the world. They were going to be flying the Concorde Supersonic aircraft from Dallas to Paris, France. They flew Boeing-747 aircraft to not only American destinations but also Europe, Mexico, Hawaii, and South America. Southwest was a smaller regional carrier flying only Boeing-737 aircraft and did not fly out of the U.S. Hmm...Paris or Lubbock? I chose Braniff International Airways. I joined them in August, 1978.

Braniff was growing rapidly because the Braniff president, Harding Lawrence, believed that in the future, there would be only about five major carriers; and he was going to make sure Braniff was one of them. So Braniff was buying aircraft and adding gates at cities all around the world. I received my brown uniform, my blue uniform, and my navigation bag—I was ready to go. I just needed to pass a Boeing-727 simulator test.

I went into the simulator and promptly failed my first test because while dealing with another emergency I had disregarded a fuel management issue. In the Boeing 727 the flight engineer was responsible to move the fuel between different fuel tanks located in the aircraft. I had allowed the fuel to move from one part of the aircraft into a wing and that was a big problem.

OK! I studied and prepared and took my second simulator. The flight was going very well when the instructor gave me three emergencies, and while dealing with them, I looked up and realized I had done it again. I failed again. One more failure and I would lose my job. In the first year with an airline you were not protected by the pilots union, so one more failure and I was done.

Susan and Ty and I had moved into an apartment in Dallas. I was not flying with the Reserves yet. If I failed again, we would be screwed. I asked myself, "How could this be happening to me?"

I finally went in for my final simulator ride. I was super prepared and was nailing everything, as they were flooding me with emergencies. I was working along solving one of the emergencies when an intuitive red warning went off in my head and I looked up and in shock and horror realized I had almost let the fuel problem happen again. I solved it and soon the simulator flight was over. I had passed and was now officially cleared to start flying as a Braniff Boeing 727 Flight Engineer.

Braniff was a very colorful airline. While I was with them they began painting their aircraft in what they called Mercedes colors and they were beautiful and classy colors. Also all the aircraft featured luxurious leather seats in both the first class and economy sections. The rumor was that one of the countries that Braniff flew into in South America could only pay so much money and so instead bartered to pay with leather. The flight attendants wore nice dresses and the pilots wore uniforms with white shirts and ties, all designed by Halston as part of Braniff's "Elegance Campaign". I soon found out that all the Braniff aircraft were extremely safe, with many backup systems and excellent pilots. Of course, each of the pilots was different. One Captain had a reputation for landing and stopping the aircraft very quickly so he could turn off at the first available taxiway and thereby always clock into a destination on time or early. I flew with him and he was a little ridiculous on stopping the aircraft quickly and taxiing very fast to the gate, but we were always on time. I actually liked him because he was one of the Captains that asked me if I wanted to fly a leg. I said, "Sure", and so he had me trade with the First Officer. I got to take off, fly the leg, and land the aircraft. I loved it.

In the meantime, Susan and I had decided to build our Captain's house and so picked out a contractor and started building a house out in the country. I also decided that I would trade in my little red Austin Healey 3000 for a used but beautiful 1971 Jaguar XKE. That Jag was sweet and fast, and turned heads, but it only had one problem: It broke down every time we drove it. It got so bad that Susan wouldn't ride with me in the Jag. A year later I sold it, with a lesson learned.

Thinking about the Jaguar also reminds me of an ice storm that blew into Dallas one winter. I was returning from a trip to Panama where it had been over ninety degrees. We landed and there was snow and ice on the Dallas runway. That was extremely unusual. I took the tram out to my Jag. I had left the XKE under a cloth car cover. Walking over to my car I saw flight attendants in their light dresses taking off their high heeled shoes and tapping on their door handles to try to break the ice. When I found my car, the cloth car cover had about two inches of ice covering the entire car. I asked a couple of passing pilots to help me and we took the cover off the car and laid it on its back. It looked like an ice duplicate of the XKE body. I stomped it down and tried to cram it into the Jag's trunk. I drove home marveling at all the Dallas drivers in their rear wheel drive pickups, with no weight in their truck beds, driving as if everything was normal... and watching them slide off the road.

One time I was on a flight to Columbia, South America and we landed at Bogota. After landing we spent an uneventful night in this interesting city. The next day we returned to the aircraft and started our flight checks. One of my jobs as the flight engineer was to compare our fuel load, runway length, elevation and temperature to a checklist table and determine what our V1, VR and V2 speeds were.

V1 speed is the speed at which the takeoff should not be aborted. If you had a serious problem before V1 you aborted. After V1 you don't have enough runway to stop so you are committed to take off. VR was the speed at which the aircraft could be rotated for takeoff. V2 was the speed that if you lost an engine the aircraft could still take off safely. Every commercial airline uses those terms.

I did my calculations, and then seeing the results, repeated the calculations, and as we were taxiing out to the runway I finally called over to the Captain and said.

"Captain, we have a problem. We are too heavy to make a takeoff!"

He was very unhappy with that and said, "Give me that."

He took my calculations and reworked them. Then he handed it back to me and said, "You're right, we have to get rid of some fuel."

The problem was that Bogota is over eight thousand feet elevation. Three thousand feet higher than the Denver Airport which is typically considered one of the highest in the United States. We taxied back in and told the ground crew how much fuel they had to download. Neither Braniff ground control nor our passengers were happy. We then taxied back out to the runway.

When cleared for takeoff, the Captain maneuvered the 727 so that we were at the very beginning of the runway with the tail of the aircraft hanging out over the end of the runway. He then put the throttles to one hundred percent, let the engines spool up until the aircraft was literally shaking, and then suddenly released the brakes. The aircraft began to accelerate slowly. When we hit V1 we were committed. It didn't look like enough runway was left. When we hit VR and the Captain began to lift the nose, I could no longer see the end of the runway in front of us. I don't know how much runway was left when we finally clawed our way into the air, but it was the only time in my entire flying career when I was unsure we had enough runway to takeoff. Sheesh.

At the same time I was getting comfortable with Braniff, the house construction was taking forever, and I was getting concerned because we mistakenly had signed a lending contract that didn't contain a rate lock-in. In other words, if the building takes longer and the bank interest rate goes up, we pay the difference. The interest rates climbed from 8.98 percent up to 12.2 percent in less than a year during our house construction. When we finally closed on the house we had no savings, but we were in our beautiful new Captain's house.

Although flying incidents were almost non-existent in the 727, I did have one very interesting experience. I was flying as flight engineer on a flight that was to land at Portland International Airport. As we approached the field, the Captain called for the landing gear to be lowered. The First Officer lowered the gear handle but the indicators in the cockpit showed that one section of the three landing gear were not down and locked. The checklist for that emergency called for me to take some action while the Captain flew a go around with the aircraft and we flew out away from the airport.

My job was now to grab a flashlight and open the cockpit door and walk back to about where the wings joined the fuselage. There I was to get down on my knees and pull up the floor carpet and look through a small, round Plexiglas view port to see if the landing gear appeared to be down and locked. Of course, people were watching me, as they had likely never seen this before. Nevertheless, no one asked me any questions. They just watched. I thought the gear looked locked, so I wandered back, trying to look professional and calm, shut the cabin door, and report my findings to the Captain. He decided to make a low pass over the airport and have other airline crews tell him what they saw. Two pilots thought it looked OK but the third was not sure.

Now we went to the next step, which was to start dumping all unnecessary fuel, and inform the passengers of our situation. They are then to begin to prepare for a crash landing which means they take things out of their pockets and are told when landing they will assume the crash position, and brace for a potential impact.

We began our final approach and in this case, the cockpit door was to be left open. Since I was sitting sideways, I could look forward as we began our landing, but when I looked back into the passenger section, I believed I saw about two hundred and eighty eyeballs looking into the cockpit and at me. We called, "brace for landing." Then the Captain made a smooth landing and we made a normal rollout. The passengers began cheering and clapping.

After we parked the aircraft, we stood by the cockpit to apologize to the passengers for the scare and the late arrival. The passengers wouldn't have any of that. They were hugging us, shaking our hands and telling us what a great crew we were. I learned that day that when people think they are going to die soon, and then they don't, they are suddenly in a jubilant mood and just happy to be alive.

On July 4th, 1980 I was informed that I had been furloughed from Braniff immediately. At that time I had more than thirty three percent of the pilot population junior to me. No airline had ever cut so deep. I was stunned. I had a new house I was trying to afford, and no savings. I had a pregnant wife with a new daughter on the way. Yes, I had begun flying with the Snakes in June, but I had only been with Braniff for two years. One of those years I had been on probation, which meant for one year I made practically nothing in salary. I was thirty two years old, and I knew that other airlines would not hire someone at that advanced age.

You might wonder why Braniff failed. They were caught in a perfect storm. They had bought the new aircraft, and the gates, and had taken huge loans. Deregulation had occurred and new small airlines were springing up. There was a fuel shortage and fuel prices had doubled in the course of one year. American Airlines had moved their Headquarters from New York City to Dallas, and had begun matching the Braniff scheduled flights all over the country, and thereby reducing the Braniff passenger load. Finally, the interest rate on the loans they had taken out soared. They could not get any additional loans, and Braniff just simply ran out of cash.

So my short commercial airline career had ended. I enjoyed Braniff, but thought the flying was a little boring as a Flight Engineer. I never got to move from my Flight Engineer position, so my experience was very limited. I never tried to work for another airline. However, I did watch Southwest Airlines prosper for the next forty years and think, "What if?"

PART SIX

Shadow's Friends: Other Pilots and Friends Share Their Stories

CHAPTER FOURTEEN

CASINO TALES

This chapter Contributed by Shadow's squadron mate, call sign—Casino, while both were serving in the Cowboys

I had been flying with the Cowboys for a few years after nearly a decade of flying Phantoms with the Marines all over the world. I was really enjoying my life working with Southwest Airlines as a Pilot and being happily married with kids; but what I really loved was flying with the Cowboys and particularly Air Combat Maneuvering (ACM). I had been fortunate as a young pilot to have flown with the VMFA-323 Snakes under Lancer, and that provided me the opportunity to fly a lot of ACM with some of the best pilots and RIOs in the Navy and Marine Corps.

By the time I got to the Cowboys I knew what I was doing, and I felt very comfortable in flying the Phantom to the edge of the envelope. To be successful in ACM with the Phantom you had to learn to fly a high speed vertical flight, but sooner or later the fight would degenerate into a slow speed brawl and that is where I felt I excelled. To be in a slow speed fight with the nose being held straight up and the airspeed falling off so that the bird was right on the edge of stalling was where I loved to fly.

One day I was in the Cowboy Ready Room and HJ wandered in and asked me an unusual question.

"Casino, would you be willing to fly an ACM hop in my backseat?"

HJ was an experienced and excellent pilot and I was a little confused so I said, "Sure, I guess. But why?"

HJ grinned and said, "Casino, I just want you to ride with me and if you see something that I'm doing wrong or something I can improve when flying ACM—I just would like you to help me out a little."

I responded, "HJ, I don't know what I can possibly show you, but it sounds fun so let's do it."

A couple of days later we were put on the schedule to go fly a one versus one ACM hop against another good Cowboy Phantom pilot and RIO.

We got our gear on and wandered out to our bird. It felt very weird to not climb into the pilot ejection seat, but to instead go back and climb into the RIO's ejection seat. I had flown in the back seat of the Phantom a few times before but it still felt uncomfortable, so I was trying to familiarize myself with all the dials and gauges as we started the aircraft up and taxied out to the end of the runway.

We did a section takeoff which was fun for me because typically I would be the lead pilot and lead the wingman (or be the wingman) and I would have to concentrate during the takeoff. Today, however, I was in the back seat of the lead aircraft... so I could just enjoy the sensation and the view as HJ lit the burners and we thundered down the runway with just a few feet separating the aircraft. I have to say that I really enjoyed that takeoff.

Soon we were into the warning area and "taking our separation" so that we could do a radar intercept before we engaged in the ACM fight. We turned in towards Dash Two being flown by Pork and Smokey. I did my best to get a radar lock on Pork. Unfortunately I was not a RIO, so I failed. Fortunately though, HJ got a Talley HO on Pork when we had a few miles separation. HJ quickly turned beak on beak, and we did a high speed pass. Pork went by so close that the canopy rattled! HJ pulled into Pork, and the fight was on.

Pork was an excellent dog fighting pilot and always very aggressive, so soon we were flying in a big vertical fight that gradually was getting smaller and slower. From time to time I would use our between cockpit Mic to tell HJ to break port or starboard or raise or lower the nose or do something with the throttles. Once when getting very slow, I told him to lower the flaps to one half. That would give you a little more lift, and if the other aircraft didn't match you it would allow you to fly a little slower and keep your nose up. Hopefully, the other aircraft would finally have to drop the nose to pick up airspeed, so that after a short delay you could drop YOUR nose; and you would now be behind him and lining up for a shot. With that move the fight would soon be over.

We fought about three fights and then we called Bingo fuel and started back to the base. While flying back, HJ and I talked about the fights and he said, "Casino, thank you! That was interesting. You didn't really tell me to do anything I was not already going to do, but you always said it a half second or second before I was ready to do it. That gained me a big advantage in each fight. You are just seeing and sensing what should be done a little quicker than I do. That was shit hot. I'm also glad we kicked Pork's butt!"

A typical fighter aircraft landing started with what was called a "break" over the field. Normally when we would come into the break we would line up with the runway we were going to eventually land on, and be level at about 1,500 feet above the ground at around 350 knots. Halfway down the runway, we would suddenly lower the wing and begin to pull 3 to 4 G banks until we were level and going the opposite direction. Once the aircraft slowed below 200 knots, we would lower the landing gear and then start lowering the flaps for landing. As we passed the end of the runway off our 3 O'clock (or 9 o'clock) position, we would begin to swoop down to a landing at a little under 145 knots. Typically a simple maneuver done after every flight.

However, because this particular day had HJ flying with me in the back seat and Pork on his wing, HJ decided to put on a little show. I was looking down in the RIO cockpit trying to turn off the unfamiliar switches and didn't notice we were not going 350 knots; we were going over 500 knots. My head was still down when suddenly HJ didn't pull four G's, he pulled six! I wasn't expecting it, and with my head down when the six G's hit I instantly went unconscious for the first time in my life. I guess several seconds passed before I started to regain consciousness. As my eyes began to open I only had clouded vision. I started trying to figure out where I was and what was happening. With my head angled down looking at an unfamiliar view from the back seat I realized I was in a Phantom, but it seemed to me that we were in an unusual attitude. We were banking down to land now and all I could see was the ground and our nose angled down. As my eyes became clearly focused I became certain in my dazed state that we were about to crash. My instincts and training told me we had to get out of the aircraft and fast. I began to sit up and reach for the ejection handle. I put my hands on the handle between my legs.

If I pulled that handle both canopies would be opened and leave the aircraft, closely followed by both ejection seats firing. HJ and I would be rocketed out of the aircraft. However, because we were in a bank, we would not be shot higher into the air. Instead, we would be shot out parallel or even angled down at the ground. In this situation I knew we would have minimum time for the ejection seats to leave the aircraft and then for us to separate from our ejection seats. It was a whole other consideration that we may not have enough time for our personal chutes to open before hitting the lake or the ground.

Just as I began the pull I heard HJ receiving clearance to land and I fully realized we were absolutely fine and would soon be doing a normal landing. I removed my hands from the ejection handle and took a deep breath as I also fully realized that I had just about ejected HJ and I from a PERFECTLY GOOD PHANTOM, and thereby, putting both our lives and careers at risk!

We taxied into the line and HJ shut down the engines. We crawled out of the aircraft and HJ pulled off his helmet, gave me a huge smile, put out his hand and said, "Thank You Casino. That was fun and I appreciate you being my RIO for a day. How did you like the break?"

I looked him in the eye and replied with a grin, "I'll never forget it!"

Back when I was a First Lieutenant in VMFA-323 I was on the schedule to fly a one versus one versus one ACM hop with Jumper and Shadow. My RIO was Spider who had over two hundred combat missions and was an excellent, experienced RIO. When we got out to the aircraft and started it up, we noticed that the aircraft had a problem and we had to shut it down. Spider and I jumped out of the aircraft and ran into the maintenance hangar where we were assigned another bird. Meanwhile, we saw Jumper and Shadow doing a section take off to go fly in the warning area off San Clemente Island. The original plan was to fly the mission and then swoop down into Miramar Naval Air Station, known as Fighter Town, and spend the night. We rushed through our preflight and got the aircraft started, then taxied out and took off to the Warning Area. As soon as we were out over the water we plugged in the burners and called Jumper to try to join the fight. Unfortunately they had already completed the fight and were going into Miramar.

Since we had nothing else to do I asked Spider if he had ever been Mach Two or two times the speed of sound. He simply said, "No!"

So I plugged in the afterburners and we started to accelerate. We were in an F-4N clean Phantom which was one of the faster Phantoms made. Gradually the Mach indicator started climbing, Mach one point two, Mach one point three, Mach one point four. It was slowly climbing but at about Mach one point six I suddenly ask Spider, "Have you ever been above fifty thousand feet?"

Spider replied, "No."

Taking that as a "Yes" to go ahead, I begin to lift the nose of the phantom up fifteen degrees. We began to climb rapidly. The altimeter was almost spinning as we climbed up through fifty thousand feet, then fifty two thousand, then fifty four thousand. It became quiet in the cockpit. Yes, the view was magnificent, and you could actually see the curvature of the earth. However, there was one big problem that we both knew existed, but neither of us acknowledged. The NATOPs manual said to never exceed fifty thousand feet of altitude. The reason was that if you lost cockpit pressurization or lost your canopy at that altitude and you weren't wearing a pressure suit and helmet, you would be dead. We were now flying in the death zone.

To make things worse, we were unfortunately still going up. I started to push the stick forward but at that speed and altitude the stick had little effect. I wanted to bring the throttles out of afterburner but knew at that altitude if I came out of burners the engines would likely flame out which would not be good at all. We kept climbing through sixty thousand feet as I kept pushing the stick down to try to get the aircraft to head down rather than up. We went through sixty three thousand, then sixty five thousand and finally we topped off at sixty seven thousand feet, or almost thirteen miles high! The view was like the view from a low satellite.

At this point we were simply a bullet that began to dive steeply. I still had little control of the aircraft. I also could not bring the throttles out of afterburner, so now our airspeed began to climb once again. Mach one point two, Mach one point four, Mach one point six. We were now starting to get a few warning lights, and the most critical one was the **low fuel light.** We were still in afterburner and headed AWAY from Miramar. We went through Mach two and quit accelerating at Mach two point two, or just under seventeen hundred miles per hour.

As we got below forty thousand feet I came out of afterburner and pulled it back to idle while banking the aircraft towards Miramar. We were now very low on fuel and a long way from the closest base, Miramar. In turning the aircraft, we began coasting down using our speed and excessive altitude to try to make it back to Miramar with enough fuel to land. We had just enough fuel (and pride) to not declare a low fuel emergency, but instead came into the break and landed safely.

To this day, I've never talked to another Phantom pilot that has flown faster nor higher than we did that day. As I was taxiing in, I was thinking that I had only asked Spider to answer two questions. With that, I had nearly killed him with excess speed, excess altitude, and low fuel. Spider had well over one thousand hours in the aircraft and over two hundred combat missions, and he had just had a brand new idiot first lieutenant almost cancel his ticket. That night at the Miramar bar I treated Spider to a steak dinner and all the booze he could handle.

CHAPTER FIFTEEN

DOG BREATH'S TALES

This chapter Contributed by Shadow's squadron mate, call sign—Dog Breath, while both were serving in the Cowboys

For thirty-five years the F-4 Phantom was regarded as the most powerful fighter jet in the US arsenal. What gave it such power were two jet engines, the J-79s built by General Electric. The advantage it gave the pilot and RIO was the capability to raise the nose, put the airplane on its tail, push in the afterburners and climb, and climb, and climb.

Like all other aspects of flying high performance aircraft, perfection of any maneuver is about "feel." It is almost more art than discipline. Good pilots have discipline, great pilots have feel, and a very few pilots have both. One of those was Casino who was exceptionally adept at vertical, slow speed flight. I was always happy to fly as Casino's RIO.

Why? Casino had a pulse rate of 45! This meant that events that the normal person would process in real time, he processed them at half the speed. Flying at Mach 1 plus, his brain could process the flight conditions, mission pursuit, and spatial orientation in the same mental state as most people counting pencils.

It was a Saturday morning back in 1983 when Casino and I, as reserve air crew, met in the VMFA-112 Ready Room to get a briefing on our mission. During the week, a call came in from a Reserve Army command in northern Louisiana. The unit would be staging simulated ground warfare and wanted to gain the experience of calling in air support and have practice ordinance delivered on a pretend aggressor force. They wanted the best in the business so they "called in the Marines".

The mission was simple. The troops would be protecting a hilltop surrounded by imaginary combatants. We would be carrying blue bombs, small ordinance with enough of a charge in the nose to make visible puff of smoke when placed on target. We would be carrying enough blue bombs for a total of 6 runs placing the ordinance on targets marked by smoke.

It was a perfect day for this exercise with little wind and clear skies. The time to target would be less than 20 minutes, giving us at least 25 minutes on target then 20 minutes back. We carried a single centerline tank just to give us extra fuel to play with. It was a rarity to get to play with the Army and we were excited to show how the Marines took care of business.

Normally when flying to a working area we stayed on positive control with the FAA controllers until we reached our destination. The routes were standardized and typically the controllers assigned our flight levels. It falls under the heading of IFR flight rules, meaning Instrument Flight Rules. We, however, filed a VFR or Visual Flight Rules flight plan. So once we were directed clear of the departing commercial flights coming east out of DFW airport, we were on our own and cleared to fly any altitude 18,000 feet and below, and any airspeed we wanted. It was like giving bank robbers the keys to the vault!

I had flown in Casino's back seat many times, and he was like all the reserve pilots. I was comfortable with their capabilities.

Despite the uncanny tendencies to throw the F-4 around the sky, they were safe, very safe. In fact, during the eight years I was a VMFA-112 Cowboy, we were totally accident free. This warranted us the coveted Ross Safety Award given by the Marine Corps to those squadrons achieving the highest standards of safety.

Now having said this, it does not mean that we did not stretch the edges of aerodynamic risk, and that is where Casino lived—right on the edge! So once we crossed over East Texas and found the Red River, we headed straight up the river north to our rendezvous point. About halfway up I felt the nose of the airplane being pushed over and a fairly rapid descent down to an altitude of under 1000 ft. After a quick leveling off, Casino rolled the plane inverted and said, "Let's see how many boaters we can wave to!" Now the F-4 can only stay inverted for about 38 seconds before all the oil is displaced out of the places it should be, into places it should not. I think we rolled back to level flight at 37.5 seconds. Ah, Casino, what a fun guy to fly with!

Our rendezvous point was a place where the Red River made a sharp turn to the west. At that point I switched our radio over to the assigned frequency and made a call to the FAC, or Forward Air Control, point person code name Rattler.

"Army Rattler, Army Rattler this is Cowboy Zero-One. We are on station and waiting for instructions."

"Roger, Cowboy, we have a visual. Turn to a heading of zero-four-zero and confirm the smoke on our first target"

"Roger, Rattler we are turning and looking."

Immediately Casino comes up on the inter-cockpit mic. "I got a tally on the smoke, Dog Breath, 2 o'clock. Let's do a low-level delivery and then we'll get into a pattern around the hill."

"Rattler 1, we have a visual on your smoke and will be making a straight in delivery. How much return fire can we expect from the bad guys?"

"Negative on ground-to-air capabilities."

The smoke was on the west side of the river about halfway up the hill. Casino pushed our speed up to five hundred knots and leveled the Phantom off at five hundred feet, not much higher than the tops of the tallest pine trees. The smoke was coming from a large clearing. Once I felt the first blue bomb detach from underside of the belly, Casino made a sharp turn to the right and rolled the plane just enough so that we could see the puff of white smoke slightly to the left of Rattler's smoke.

"Direct hit Cowboy Zero-One. Standby for target two."

Within ten seconds we picked up the second plume of red smoke but this time, instead of a level delivery, we gave the troops a little excitement as we climbed to 12,000 feet, rolled the airplane inverted, steadied on a heading that paralleled the direction of blowing smoke, and settled into about a thirty degree dive angle...or maybe closer to forty degrees. As we were hurling ourselves in what feels like a straight down trajectory toward the target at four hundred and fifty knots, I called out our altitudes, " 10,000, 9,000, 8,000, standby, Mark." At about 7,500 feet, Casino dropped two bombs this time. Again we rolled the Phantom just enough to see that the puffs of white smoke were close enough for the simulated kill.

"Another good hit Cowboy Zero-One, my spotter confirms at least ten bad guys down".

In the background we could hear some cheers and "ooh-rahs".

For the next 10-15 minutes we continued our mission. They would pop the smoke on the targets and we'd drop a blue bomb while lighting up the sky with eye-popping twists and turns accented by the thundering noise of the J-79's. We also noticed that as our proficiency to deliver on target improved, their smoke targets were getting closer to the real troops. Finally, in a grand finale, we put our left wing down and circled around their hilltop just below the ridge, moving counterclockwise from a 9 o'clock to a 12 o'clock position. We could clearly see the troops in their tactic positions, a large tent camp, a long row of porta-potties, and a semi-circle of tables probably used for training sessions and chow. Not sure anyone could see me clearly, but I was doing my best homecoming wave!

As we pulled off the last target, again receiving the cheers and adulation of the soldiers, Casino informed me we were at "Bingo," telling us it was time to go home.

"Rattler 1, Rattler 1, Cowboy is at Bingo fuel. Great work you guys." A few seconds went by when suddenly we heard a new voice coming from their communications center.

"Cowboys, Colonel Meyers here. You boys did a shit hot job, and we thank you but..."

"Here it comes," Casino said to me, knowing all too well what would be coming next.

The colonel continued, "...the troops want to know if you could give us a show?"

"Roger that" Casino broadcast to them, "hold onto your shorts!"

We vectored the aircraft at a much slower speed out to the north east about five miles from the hill and started a slow turning descent that would eventually put the nose of the Phantom on the center of the camp. We were also at eye level to a plateau where the Army had elaborately set up camp.

"Ready, Dog Breath", Casino eagerly asked.

"Let's do it," I said.

Suddenly I could feel the winding of our J-79 engines. In moments we accelerated from three hundred and fifty to six hundred knots with our nose still on the center of the camp; only now Casino brought us below the height of the hill. The soldiers were now watching this mechanical dagger below their eye level hurling at them at speeds they likely could not comprehend. What was probably eerie to them, was the absence of sound, even as we got closer. I am certain that many were convinced we would ram into the side of the hill, and kill everyone.

Then it came. First the double boom and being thrust back into my seat; then the deafening noise. We had engaged the afterburners turning the F-4 from a fighter jet into a swept wing rocket! We had released the Beast.

"OK," Casino said, "let's give them their show".

At that moment, the nose of the F-4, still in afterburner, abruptly pitched up straight into the sun. At that same moment, since Casino had timed this vertical maneuver directly over the camp, all hell was breaking loose!

We stayed in a near perfect vertical flight path until we reached seventeen thousand feet. At that altitude Casino pulled back on the afterburner and we started to level off. All during our climb I was looking in the rear view mounted outside my canopy.

"Hey, Casino, I think that maybe we might have blown a few Army grunts off the hill".

Casino, who had also been watching, clicked his cockpit mic, gave me laugh and said, "Dog Breath, I think we blew them ALL off the hill."

"Roger that," I responded with a slightly fiendish giggle. I then proceeded to get back to work, forgetting about our mission and concentrating on getting us home.

"Rattler 1, Rattler 1, this is Cowboy Zero-One departing the working area. Thanks for the work."

We waited for a response, but the only transmission we heard was a faint "click, click." We switched to the last assigned frequency given to us by flight control.

"Dallas Center, Dallas Center, this is Cowboy Zero-One. We are back on-line and awaiting instructions to Navy Dallas".

"Roger, Zero-One, we have you. Turn to a heading of two-zero-zero, maintain present altitude, and contact Approach Control on 234.7".

"Zero-One, turning and switching".

The rest of the flight home was rather boring. We received vectors from Approach Control, were turned over to Navy Tower, and though we were not really sure we had dispensed of all our little blue bombs, made a nice easy, straight-in, approach and landing. Mission complete, we had saved the soldiers from their aggressors and lived to fight another day (and we got to have some fun!). As we pulled into the line and Casino let the engines wind down, I recalled a Steve Martin quote from his first comedy album where he proudly boasts to the audience, in a sing-song manner, "I...get paid...for doing THIS!"

Post log

Two weeks later, the squadron had its weekend drill. Casino and I were leisurely walking down the hall, coffee mugs in hand, when our Commanding Officer beckoned us into his office. As we stood before him, not being invited to sit down, he silently handed us a letter that also contained two pictures. We looked at the pictures first.

One showed a young Captain in his Army combat fatigues with his right arm in a sling. The other, put everything into perspective, and while we both wanted to laugh, we weren't sure how this was going to play out with the CO. We both remained attentive and serious, and neither showed our natural reactions to what we saw.

The picture, likely taken very shortly after our final act at Red River, showed their tent city in serious disarray. Porta-potties laying on their side, and their training and chow facilities just discombobulated with half of the tables that served chow blown over and the other half cobbled together in a pile. It looked like a tornado had swept through the camp, but we knew who had caused the disruption. The letter went on to say:

October 20, 1983

"Dear Cowboy 01,

We first want to thank you for your excellent simulation of close air support. Our troops learned a great deal from the experience. You are to be commended for your proficiency in putting your bombs on our smoke to neutralize the aggressors. This in a timely and accurate manner. However, your final fly over, which we anticipated to be a slow and easy flight over our camp with a few wing rocks to acknowledge our troops, turned into something very different.

When you chose to put your aircraft in vertical climb while going full throttle on your engines it was perfectly timed to occur directly over the center of our camp. Now we are not suggesting that you did this on purpose but it put Bravo Company into a total state of chaos! It took us the rest of the day to bring some semblance of order, as men had to first retrieve tents, chairs, and recover about a half dozen of our men who had been blown down the Hill, to put our camp back together! Fortunately, we only had to send three men to sick bay for bruises and some minor joint damage. The tents, porta-potties, tables, and chairs did not fare so well.

We have learned two great lessons from this experience. The first: NEVER ask reserve Marine fighter crews to "put on a show!" Second: Next time, use Army helicopters; not as exciting, but far more controllable.

Sincerely yours,

Major F. P. Waters,
Battalion commander
47th Louisiana National Guard
Camp Beauregard
Pineville, LA

Once we had read the letter and started to speak, the CO put up his hand to silence us. After a few seconds, he said, "I am going to keep this letter, as I know that despite your great humility, copies would soon be hanging on the Ready Room wall as trophies, and a tribute to your great prowess at being morons. You are dismissed."

As we left the CO's office, Casino grinned and broke the silence. "If they can't take a joke, f*** them!"

"Roger that!" was my only reply. We never spoke of it again!

CHAPTER SIXTEEN

FLEET'S TALES TWO

This chapter Contributed by Shadow's squadron mate, call sign—Fleet, while both were serving in the Cowboys

I arrived at the VMFA-112 Cowboys just after the squadron transitioned from the aging, single seat, (but lethal) F-8 Crusader.

There was a lot to overcome. The biggest challenge was to get the old, hard-headed, single seater pilots into the newer, more lethal, more modern, two seater F-4 Phantom.

It didn't bother me, as there was already a good RIO stationed there whom I knew pretty well and he was very good. He warmly welcomed me and gave me the thumb nail version of what to expect and from whom.

I wasn't worried. I had recently left the active duty Marine Corps and had one hundred and thirty one combat missions under my belt. I was a Captain, USMCR, and I knew how to avoid taking shit from unwanted sources, regardless of rank. I had learned how to handle that in Nam Phong, Thailand, otherwise known as The Rose Garden.

Almost all the "Old Farts," what we called the older pilots, were pretty good guys. They liked to fly and by then were proven aviators. They were just new to the two-seat fighter and unsure as to what a RIO could do for them. Or frankly, what the airplane could do; like going Mach Two vs. Mach One. They were used to flying their own airplane, doing their own talking over the air, and doing their own navigating.

In the Phantom, it was the RIO who had control of the radar set which enabled the use of the longer range Sparrow missile. The RIO also conducted most of the communication outside the aircraft, and were responsible for navigation.

The older ones also had to learn how to fly air-to-air successfully by making the best use of a second set of knowing eyeballs in the back seat. The F-4 handled differently than the F-8, and salty RIO's knew better than the pilots when the plane was being put in a position that could become "iffy" or outright dangerous.

Most were willing to listen, especially when we were in dog shit weather and they had their hands full of new airplane. But there were always a few that just had to fly into a poop sandwich, and then let a RIO help get them out. However, once converted, it was those pilots that sang the loudest to the choir of hard-heads.

One pilot in particular comes to mind. Great big man, call sign withheld here. In real life a pilot for the old Continental Airlines. Early in his fam/transition hops, I was scheduled to fly with him. After a normal brief, we went out to mount up and launch. It was a clear day and we were basically going to bore holes in the sky. Not a big deal, other than doing a few things pilots needed to know how to do and becoming comfortable with doing it in the Phantom. A "high rudder reversal" was one of the better ways to get the older F4s to turn when it was low on speed and energy but needed to get the nose pointed back at a bogey.

But first we had to taxi out, check in, and get takeoff permission. We were cleared onto the active runway and started engine run-ups. Then the pilot began going down the pre-takeoff checklist. Regardless of the experience level, in the F-4 those were always done. Mandatory.

The pilot ran through the checklist and I watched and listened. He then told me he was ready to go. I said, "No we aren't. You forgot something".

"What?" he yelled.

From the backseat, a RIO can visually see if the flaps are in fact down, as they are supposed to be for takeoff. Otherwise, the nose of the airplane would suddenly jump up, and the plane could stall if not caught immediately.

No-flap takeoffs ARE allowed, if they were pre-briefed. The pilot just has to be aware that the nose is going to go up—fast.

I told the pilot to check flap position. Then I heard an "Aw shit". He had read the checklist and had forgotten to set the flaps. Once they were positioned, we had a normal take-off and flew an uneventful hop.

He did fine in the rickety part of the hop, nose-high rudder reversals, and flew smoothly in an unusual attitude.

On the way back, he asked sheepishly, "Can we keep that to ourselves?"

I answered, "Yes, but it will cost you two beers!"

Then there was a pilot with the call sign Crazy. Crazy and I were from the same part of south Texas. We even knew some of the same people. He had the call sign "Crazy" given to him because he had started in aviation flying crop dusters. Low and crazy flying, as in under power lines to get the poison spray on the crops.

We were at a place called 29 Palms, in Arizona. This Marine expeditionary field had a very short landing strip at that time. It was a runway made of Marston matting, not concrete. Our job was to take our bird, single ship, over to El Toro, California, where the rest of the squadron was currently located.

It was a scorching day in a very hot place and Crazy had a mild case of get there-itis. A hotter than hell day, a short runway that ran off a cliff at the departure end, and a crazy crop duster pilot. What could possibly go wrong?

Typically, Phantoms taking off out of 29 Palms either used the catapult launch, or just lightly fueled their Phantoms so they could take off in a short distance. Instead we snuck around avoiding the heavies (senior Marine aviators) that we knew were doing their two weeks active time. We had the plane loaded with more than normal fuel, but just enough to make it to El Toro, and not much more. Crazy told me he had looked up the field length, winds, temperature, aircraft weight etc. in the bible (NATOPS chart) and that we could do it.

So we mounted up, taxied, and got cleared for takeoff. We pulled onto the runway and went into full afterburner. We started accelerating, but it felt too slow. I was watching the thousand foot markers flick by and the nose of the bird was not going upward like it normally would. I realized that we had probably made a fatal mistake. We didn't have enough airspeed and we were about out of runway.

As the end of the runway passes under our nose, I felt about 5 G's come on the airplane. On tower frequency I heard a garbled transmission mention something about "trouble." The unusual 5 G pullup barely launched the aircraft off the ground, and the bird did not sink back to the ground, **because we WERE now going over the cliff edge!** We began descending and accelerating in full afterburner. I felt more G's come on as I twisted around, only to see a desert dirt rooster tail being created by our afterburners, as we were flying down the hill, but still very low to the ground. Finally we gained enough speed and begin to climb safely up to altitude.

We made it to El Toro laughing all the way. Later, at the bar, the Lt. Colonel from our squadron who had watched our take off at 29 Palms cornered us. He was pissed off.

"Didn't you hear me, you assholes?"

I told him I had a broken transmission and we were busy at the time.

He said, "I told you two to eject!"

Crazy looked at me with his shit eating grin and said,

"Good thing we didn't!"

"You'd have a hell of a time explaining why two guys jumped out of a perfectly good airplane. An ass chewing is a piece of cake compared to that."

He left in a huff. I looked at Crazy.

"OK valley boy. Your crop dusting days are over!"

He looked back at me with that grin and said,

"No they're not!"

PART SEVEN

Flying with the Best

CHAPTER SEVENTEEN

THE BACON BROTHERS

The Bacon Brothers were two of the VMFA–112 Cowboys. However, there were actually three; not REAL brothers, but brothers in the way of Call Signs and squadron camaraderie.

The Call Signs were Pork, Pig, and Pig, except that we called the second Pig, Piglet. All three were unique individuals and fine pilots, both military and later in commercial airlines. Pig actually flew combat missions in the Serbia – Croatia conflict.

Piglet was tall, slim, and typically quiet unless provoked. Piglet once saved a Marine F-4 Phantom that had a Boundary Layer Control failure (BLC) which was designed to put hot air from the engines over the wings to allow slower flight for take-off and landing. The BLC failed and the Phantom caught fire. Rather than the recommended ejection, Piglet flew the aircraft and safely landed it at Yuma Marine Air Base. For that bit of flying he received the Single Mission Air Medal, and I know of no other Cowboy who received one of those as a Cowboy.

Pig and Pork joined the Cowboys about the same time and were almost always seen together. Both were married, and both flew with the Airlines. Both loved flying and sports. Both were sneaky smart and active in the clowning around that made the Cowboys fun.

Pig was a Navy Academy graduate, although he never mentioned it. A natural athlete with a ready smile and good self-deprecating sense of humor. He had done some of the flying in the movie, *The Great Santini*, and could be spotted in the Ready Room scenes in that movie. Pig did everything smooth and with a smile. I remember the first time I met him. I had just got back into the Cowboys. I needed to go somewhere but had no car. Pig was flying with the airline and the Cowboys so he had a brand new car. He heard me asking around and loaned me his with no questions asked. He didn't know me from a hole in the ground. I never forgot that.

Pork was a unique individual. He was a former Florida bare foot water skier in a water show. I remembered him from when I was a Recruiting Officer, and he was attending ROTC as a student at the University of Texas. He would stop by our table and talk and I figured he was just another college punk with dreams of flying Phantoms. Only he ended up doing just that.

Pork was a very aggressive pilot. He was rough and abrupt with the stick, making the aircraft go where he wanted it to go. He was an excellent ACM plot. One day while flying out in the Warning area in Texas, he had a big engine panel fly off his Phantom. He kept cool and did all the right things and got the bird back to Dallas safely. I had to later go out to a county courthouse in the middle of nowhere and get permission from a magistrate to drive across a bunch of farmer's oat fields. The goal was to pick up the panel and take it back to Dallas to complete the incident investigation. Pork had the presence of mind to mark the spot on his TACAN so we basically drove right to the spot and found it.

Pork told another story of when he was flying out of an island in the pacific doing a trans-Pac. He had a failed landing main mount on take-off. He jerked the nose of the aircraft into the air and ejected. He had a good chute and landed not far from where he had just ejected. However, he was close enough to the fireball that he was singed. The ambulance came roaring over and a Navy Nurse jumped out. Pork knew her from the Officer Club. She approached him, looking at both the fireball and his singed flight suit, and asked him if he was OK.

His response was, "Pam, there is nothing wrong with me that a blowjob won't fix." He was a bachelor at the time, so everything was cool.

You may recall that Pork was the type of guy that was up for anything, anytime. You never wanted to dare him to do something. One time we were having a Cowboy Court with much drinking and laughing, but still trying to conduct an official court proceeding. Suddenly Pork spotted a big water bug roach scurrying across the floor. Pork yelled out "Fox 2!" He then grabbed the Bug in his hand and threw it into his mouth and swallowed it, immediately followed by chugging his beer.

The room went silent for a second and then erupted into astonished laughing, pointing, gagging gestures and howling at the moon. Pork had developed a reputation as someone who could and would challenge and beat anyone at eating or drinking literally anything, but now we had proof positive. Pork was just standing there smiling and laughing and drinking beer to drown the poor bug. Pork was one of a kind.

For their own reasons Pig and Pork left the Cowboys, and joined the Air Force Reserves and began flying F-16 Fighters out of Arizona. They kept all their Cowboy connections and in fact one RIO helped Pork keep his finances straight. They would bring their F-16s to Dallas and fly against the Cowboys from time to time.

They were invited to the first formal "Cowboy Dining In" that Shadow had convened. This was where the famous "General White" fiasco had occurred—that story is forthcoming. Pork sat right across the table from me with Pig right beside him as usual. I will swear, and Merle will back me up, that Pork's face was glowing that night, and not just from the wines and Port we were drinking.

The next morning Pork invited a Marine RIO Jim Bob to accompany him on a flight in his F-16. They came into the break hot after their flight, and as Pork pulled the F-16 into the break above the field, the F-16 just kept rolling right into the ground. Both were killed, and only Pork's boot and wedding ring were recovered. The word spread like wildfire that day. Everyone was stunned and extremely sad. We had lost a brother.

The next year there was another Cowboy Dining In. Pig and Merle and I sat in the same spots. We left Pork's chair empty. I screwed up my courage and told Pig I wished Pork was with us. Pig said, "He is!" and raised up a shoebox with some of Pork's things in it. We nodded and when the food fight began he placed a napkin over the box and said, "Pork would never want to miss this!"

Pig later made the rest of the Cowboys proud when he became a Major General in the Air Force Reserves. Now we called him General Pig! He still pilots fighters as an aggressor pilot against different air forces around the world. He is the oldest active fighter pilot that I know.

The Bacon Brothers were always together, and they helped make the Cowboys a formidable fighting unit. They also helped bring together the brotherhood where a good time was expected and delivered.

CHAPTER EIGHTEEN

THE COWBOYS

Going back in time, after I had managed to join Braniff Airlines, I was finally accepted into the Marine Reserves squadron that goes by the name Dallas Cowboys VMFA-112. At this point, I must implore you to understand something. I love sports (and especially football) just as much as the next guy. I am athletic myself, and can appreciate the amazing efforts and competitions of all the athletes in many different arenas. I am, of course, fully aware that the name "The Dallas Cowboys" is a famous one in the sport of football, and was even more famous in the day of their coach—Tom Landry. The Dallas Cowboys was "America's team" then. They were the most loved team in America, while at the same time ALSO being the most hated team in America. Everyone knew the Dallas Cowboys football team. However, "The Dallas Cowboys" that I was involved with was a reserve Marine fighter squadron that featured the same name, the same Cowboy "star" and the same Cowboy colors. However, we excelled in a completely different type of competition. From this point on, we will just refer to them as "The Cowboys".

The Cowboys had been transitioning from the F-8 into the F-4 Phantom and they needed experienced F-4 pilots to join them. The Cowboys were generally a few years older than me. Most had flown in Viet Nam and most flew F-8s Crusaders and only a couple had flown the F-4. They had been recruiting F-4 RIOs and some good ones had joined. The Cowboys were salty and cocky and I liked them immediately.

VMFA-112 flew out of Navy Dallas located in Grand Prairie, Texas, a suburb of Dallas. This base primarily featured the Cowboys and a C-52 helicopter squadron. The Cowboys had a large Hangar. The airfield featured an eight thousand foot runway that ended at the edge of a lake. A main street passed close to the end of one runway. It was common for cars to park near this point so they could watch the F-8s and then the F-4 Phantoms take off and land. I admit it was a show to watch either aircraft light the afterburners, especially at night. However, when the F-8 lit its afterburner there was not only flame, but an extremely loud bang like a large gun going off, and then the burner flame would emerge. It was quite an exhibition.

To be a Marine Reserve pilot, you had to fly whenever you could, but attend at least one drill per month and deploy with the squadron at least once per year. To maintain your spot in the squadron you had to fly a minimum of one hundred hours per year. You could not do that flying just on drill weekends and a single deployment. Most of the aircrew lived in the Dallas area or were airline pilots so they could get to Dallas frequently at no cost.

The squadron had a contingent of Regular Marines that worked full time at the squadron just like they would at any other active duty squadron. The squadron reported to Marine Air Group-11 and most of the Group were Active Duty, but Reserves filled many billets. Most of the pilots and RIOs were Reserves and had to dedicate a good portion of their lives to flying and supporting the squadron.

I was one of the first true F-4 Phantom Pilots to join, but I was quickly joined by other hard core, experienced pilots and RIOs, that were getting out of the Regular Marines to pursue other careers. The Cowboys had many applicants but soon became very particular on who they would bring on board. Because we could be selective and add aircrew from the West Coast, the East Coast, or Hawaii, we began adding only truly elite aircrew. Unless you had a sponsor that could vouch for both your flying and your character, you were not going to be allowed to join. One thousand hours in the F-4 was a common requirement and many of us had over two thousand hours.

What that meant was that the Cowboys soon began enhancing their already impressive reputation. The Cowboys would deploy to other active Marine and Navy bases and fly against Regular F-4 Phantom crews and A-4 Adversary aircrews and win. This was not surprising, as we typically had vastly more hours fighting in the Phantom than most aircrews we faced. The amalgamation of the new but experience F-4 pilots with the older, salty, former F-8 pilots was interesting and fun. The Skipper, XO, Ops O and AMOs were all senior reserve officers. They had call signs such as Giant, Slick, Rounder and Frank. They were very aggressive in the air and wild on the ground. They were newer to the F-4 and sometimes they flew on the edge. One deployment we watched as two of the senior aircrew in the squadron declared emergency fuel when flying from Navy Dallas to Yuma, Arizona. When they landed, one Phantom ran out of fuel while turning off the runway and the other ran out of fuel pulling into the aircraft parking area. We just shook our heads and said, "Whoooee!"

Flying out of Yuma was excellent. The runways were very long and the weather was high desert, so almost always clear. The base was surrounded by Warning Areas and gunnery ranges so that we could fly missions that called for dropping bombs, or flying ACM, or both combined on one mission. It was reasonably close to the Marine Ground Training Area called Twenty Nine Palms so we could fly missions supporting them. It was also near to Miramar Naval Air Station and Luke Air Force Base so we had plenty of Marine, Navy, and Air Force adversaries.

Whenever we deployed to Yuma it was a custom for the aircrew to go out to a specific Mexican restaurant downtown. On the walls at this restaurant were various plaques dedicated to individuals and groups that had set records while eating nachos. Their nachos were round, with cheese, and each order had a large amount of jalapeños. The contest was to eat as many nachos as possible while also drinking margaritas. I can tell you that if you have twenty Marines eating twenty to fifty jalapeños, and drinking pitchers of margaritas, you can guarantee a fun and unusual evening (with regrets the next morning). We also had a squadron golf tournament with twenty aircrew playing golf. When we got to the last hole we waited until all twenty were lined up and then we all teed off at the same time—twenty golf balls zinging around the eighteenth hole followed by a group "moon."

One of the great things about a reserve squadron is that you don't have the same turnover you have in active squadrons. That means that the same group of aircrew might fly together for five to ten years. Pilots and RIOs formed teams that typically flew together and became even more formidable. The RIOs in the squadron were smart, cocky, and as confident as the pilots. They would tell you if you were screwing up, and they would help you, if that was needed. Initially the F-8 pilots gave them a little lack of respect because they had flown their whole career in single seat aircraft. However, once you had flown with an experienced F-4 RIO that could find aircraft on the radar thirty miles out and keep bogeys off your six o'clock in a fight, they were gradually accepted and became friends with the F-8 pilots like they already were with the F-4 pilots.

One time I was leading a four ship formation and after our primary mission I asked one of the RIOs if he knew where Merle, one of the all-time great RIOs, lived. This was out in the west Texas ranch land area, and he said he could find it. Sure enough, he identified it from the air. We rolled in and made a low altitude, high speed pass with four Phantoms doing five hundred knots right over his ranch. As we pulled off we saw people come running out of the house and barn, so we made another big circle and then made another low pass and as we climbed out we hit the afterburners. We heard later that all his neighbors had called him and asked if that was his squadron saying hello and that they loved it. We are not sure if the cattle loved it quite as much.

The ACM fights in the squadron were epic, as everyone was good and no one liked to lose. I remember one fight where an F-4 pilot, Snoopy, that was going to join the Cowboys later, brought a TA-4 out to Dallas to act as an adversary. We had one engagement where Casino was flying the TA-4, with Snoopy in his back seat. Casino was elite and after a long engagement we were in a slow speed scissors. That maneuver is when both planes are headed up in a vertical climb, but with each plane rotating around the other on the way up, creating kind of a scissor pattern. Each time we would cross, we would lose a little more air speed and be a little more nose high. Finally Casino and Snoopy were behind me and closing. They were very close and almost under my Phantom. They were having a ball. Unbeknownst to them, I was so slow and so nose high, that I was on the edge of a stall; and if I stalled, the nose would likely pitch down right into them. I was doing everything I could just to keep the nose up a little longer, because they were under me. At the last moment they pulled off, and I dropped the nose right where they had been a second before. They still laugh about that fight and say they could see my eyeballs getting huge as they got closer.

Most times if the Cowboys deployed for more than a week a Cowboy Court would be planned. A Cowboy Court called for aircrew to charge other aircrew with crimes such as coming into the break too fast, or not refueling successfully on the first pass, or pulling too many G's and breaking the aircraft. The crimes could be real and serious, or trivial, or just ridiculously minor. All crimes had to be submitted to the court in a poem fashion.

Then a Cowboy Judge would lead the Court with an Assistant reading the crimes. After the reading the suspect could attempt to mount a defense (never a good idea) and the jury (all the Cowboys) would show thumbs up or thumbs down. The Judge could then make his ruling. Of course, beer was flowing and it was wild with laughing and taunting. More about this "Cowboy Court" later...

After I had been in the squadron a few years the Cowboys decided to deploy to Hawaii. I was living in Southern California at the time, so the fact that the Cowboys were staging the Trans-Pac to fly right out of El Toro MCAS in Southern California was fortunate for me. For the Marine Phantoms to make it to Hawaii they would need to meet up with a C-130 tanker several hundred miles out over the Pacific Ocean, and then meet another C-130 tanker when they were a few hundred miles from Hawaii. If you were unable to fuel on the first refueling, the plan was to have enough fuel to return to El Toro. However, if the squadron failed to meet the second tanker, it would be very serious in regards to fuel. Three times I participated in the briefs and planning for the Trans-Pac and flew out towards the tanker. Two times weather made rejoining with the tanker impossible. The third time one of our aircrew messed up on the tanker and tore the drogue off the C-130 so they could not continue. I had to fly with that aircraft back to El Toro. It was very disappointing for me, as the eventual deployment was regarded as a big success.

Every year on November 10th the Marine Corps celebrates the Marine Corps Birthday. The way they do this is by holding a Marine Corps Ball. The Ball is a formal event. All Marines wear their finest Dress Blues. The Blue uniforms are fabulous with Red stripes running down the outside of the trousers. Stiff collar. Spit shined black shoes. White Hat with gold trim and the Marine Corps emblem front and center. Medals are displayed as is your rank. Women are expected to attend in formal dresses and they do!

The Ball has certain traditions. Oftentimes there was an introduction of Marines wearing uniforms from the past two hundred years with a description of the war and role the Marines played in each conflict. There was a formal Birthday cake and an introduction of both the oldest Marine attending and the youngest Marine attending. The Commandant's Annual Birthday Celebration letter was read and some other remarks were made by the ranking Officer. Of course, the Star Bangled Banner was sung, and a small Marine Corps band played the Marine Corps Hymn.

One year we were attending the Ball in Dallas and Dog Breath's wife was to sing the National Anthem. She was an excellent singer and she looked lovely, but when the band started playing, Dog Breath looked at me in alarm and even I realized that something was amiss. The band had started the Anthem one octave higher than normal. I was not certain how she was going to hit the high note of the National Anthem and what would she do if she could not hit the note? The song was building to its dramatic high note and Dog Breath and I were holding our breath. The high note finally arrived and she hit it beautifully, if softly. I wanted to yell and clap right then, but we had to wait till the song was over. She came over to our table and we all looked at her and she said, "I think that is the highest note I have ever hit!"

It was funny then.

The Marine Corps Balls typically got a little wild and went on until late into the evening, but they were always fun, and helped remind us of why we were Marines.

Another deployment found the Cowboys at Tyndall Air Force Base in Florida. Tyndall was fun as we flew against F-106's and enjoyed the water when off duty. As the week went on we became familiar with a group of ladies who called themselves the Allied School of Sailing Sluts. They liked to drink, were attractive, and they were fun. They invited the Cowboys to join them on a large sailboat. The general idea was to sail out to an island and have a few drinks at the No Name bar and then return. It was a perfect afternoon and a great time was had at the bar. However, when sailing back with the sun setting, one Cowboy decided to jump overboard. That was funny, and the sail boat maneuvered back to pick him up when another Cowboy leaped into the water. That was also kind of funny, but a few of us more sober than others began to realize as more people went into the water that it was getting dark, and the sailboat was not a powerboat that could pick up swimmers easily. Finally we had all the Cowboys back aboard. Mention the Sailing Slut Cruise to a Cowboy and you will get a smile.

At that same deployment we had some fun in the Officers Club with the Air Force pilots that we had been flying against. They were great guys and we were having lots of fun, but they tended to be younger, since they were still on active duty while we were largely Reserves. Suddenly I heard Z-Man claiming that Killer was the strongest man in our squadron and probably the strongest man in the bar. To prove it, Z-Man announced that Killer could and would pick up at one time any three guys the Air Force squadron nominated. Now Killer was a large Marine and had played college football and he began flexing and loosening his neck muscles. Immediately the Cowboys began making bets. Some betting for Killer, and others betting against Killer. The Air

Force picked out three big pilots, each well over two hundred pounds. The betting and yelling picked up as the crowd began to form around the Air Force pilots. In order for Killer to pick them up they sat down with their knees toward Killer so he could wrap his arms around all their legs.

Z-man took Killer aside and was coaching him up and rubbing his shoulders. Meanwhile the Cowboys were making bets and ordering more beer. The bets were now close to one thousand dollars. Finally, Killer squatted down in the middle of the three pilots and wrapped his big arms around the legs of all three and he started a count down with the crowd yelling: "One...Two... Three!"

At the count of three, Killer jumped up and sprang away, while all the Cowboys poured their beer mugs full of beer on top of the Air Force pilots helplessly seated on the floor. Everyone was roaring and laughing and afterwards buying the three drowned pilots beers. That was a good time! That is known as the Three Man Lift!

After I had been with the Cowboys a few years we got another shot in the arm as Lancer became the MAG-11 Group Commander. Once again the maintenance began to improve and the Cowboys began to fly even more and more sorties. We also began flying the F-4 S which finally had smokeless engines and slats. It was a great airplane with a good radar and improved handling.

Over the years the Cowboys deployed to both Cherry Point, North Carolina and to San Clemente Island off the shore of California. Both those deployments were to test the squadron's readiness to deploy to more primitive conditions and to test the squadron's logistics capabilities. For those deployments, the Cowboys worked and slept in tents. They ate the food you would eat in combat field conditions. They coordinated planning and coordination of strategies and tactics with other ground and air units that we would have to work with in future conflicts. It reminded me of aspects of early conditions at Nam Phong, and I thought they were important deployments.

I had been flying with the Cowboys for about four years. I had served the last couple of years as the Aviation Maintenance Officer (AMO). The entire squadron was now made up of experienced F-4 Phantom pilots and RIOs. All the former F-8 pilots that had welcomed us into the squadron and that had created the winning Cowboy culture had moved on. It was our squadron now, and we were ready, but first we would have to welcome a new Commanding Officer. Gulp! It was going to be me. That is the rest of the story.

CHAPTER NINETEEN

SKIPPER

After a few years with the Cowboys I was told that I would be the next squadron Commander. That was a huge honor, and a highlight of my life. To be the squadron Commander meant now I was responsible for fifteen F-4s, all the ground equipment, the hangar, approximately forty aviators and over two hundred Marines. Susan and I were living in Chicago now with two children. I was an executive in a huge healthcare technology company with its own challenges. But now I was to be made the Skipper.

The change of Command Ceremony was emotionally moving for me as these functions are very formal, and yet I had the opportunity to speak to my squadron and share my view of what was important about what we Reserves represented. Lancer was the Group CO. Rookie became my Executive Officer, Mambel my Operations Officer, and Fleet became my Maintenance Officer. It was very strange the first few times I walked the hall and was called "Skipper". To start an AOM and have the squadron come to attention until you take your seat in the front was very different. It was fun to be able to put together my plans and goals and present them to the assembled squadron. I had a great maintenance team and exceptional flyers that were all one hundred percent F-4 trained. Those were great years for both me and the Cowboys.

I remember on one of the first deployments the guys had a birthday party for me. As part of the party, I had to stand up in front of the aviators and drink a Flaming Hooker. This is a drink that is set on fire just before you drink it. I had never had a Flaming Hooker before, but with everybody watching I couldn't say,

"No Thanks, maybe later!"

So my strategy was to throw the drink down my mouth and therefore put out the flame. HJ was standing beside me, and unbeknown to me he was holding a towel. When I threw the drink into my mouth I noticed that all the aircrew had their mouths open, staring, with shocked looks on their faces… and they were starting to point. Immediately (thankfully) HJ reached over and smothered my face with his towel. I soon learned that when I threw down the drink full of alcohol, some of it had splashed on my face and my entire face had momentarily caught fire; and my mustache was lighting up.

That reminds me of another Cowboy Court we had. I was the Judge and HJ was to be my right hand man or "the High Tribunal." We had picked up some fancy pointed hats like wizards and we both had capes, with mine being white and HJ's being black, so we were ready. We were introduced, and the Cowboy Court and all stood to attention. Of course, food and drinks were being consumed as we started reading the charge poems and listening to accusations and rebuttals. As the Court continued the crowd was having fun and feeling no pain, and after one fine was assessed, the accused threw a dinner roll at me. The roll went whizzing by and I didn't move a muscle. Someone else picked up another roll and tossed it at me and that missed also; again I didn't twitch. Pretty soon the entire room was throwing food at me and for one minute the rules of the universe were apparently suspended, because nothing could touch me sitting perfectly still in my white robe and peaked hat. HJ was getting buried while I was in a Cone of Invulnerability. Eventually I got caught with a roll dunked in water. The Cowboy Court then continued, but that night has always been remembered as the Cowboy Court with the Cone of Invulnerability.

I flew with the Cowboys for nine years. During those nine years I flew into Dallas from Los Angeles, Washington, Chicago, and Atlanta. Although it was hard on my family it was the best of times for flying. The squadron continued to bring in new and extremely talented aviators. When I flew, I knew my RIO and my wingman were going to be excellent. If we deployed, we would always do well in the exercises because we were experienced, and had flown together so much that we could predict and take advantage of the strengths of our squadron mates. It would not be unusual to be flying with Rookie, Frisco, Z-man and Mambel, all with over 2,000 hours in the Phantom, fighting against other aircraft and squadrons, and then landing and spending the evening with my friends.

During a deployment to Fallon Naval Air Station in Nevada, I had an experience I would never forget.

The squadron was flying air-to-ground sorties and I was leading a division (four), but with another division ahead of us. We were trying to find the target but there was a thick cloud layer. We kept flying lower and lower trying to keep the division ahead of us in sight. I could see the mountains on the horizon and beginning to be on both sides of our flight. I realized that we might soon be flying into a box canyon with no room to turn around to fly out. I had no choice but to motion to my wingman that we were going to raise our noses and go into the clouds. Because I didn't know how high the mountains were around us I told my wingman "Burners Now!' I engaged the afterburner and pulled the nose even higher. I glanced over and saw none of my wingmen were in sight.

This was not good! We were going almost straight up like a rocket ship—but with nothing to see except clouds. Our other three wingmen aircraft were somewhere around us, but where we did not know. My airspeed began dwindling as we kept climbing, and I began to imagine what it was going to be like if we ran out of airspeed before we came out of the clouds. If that happened, we would be doing a slow speed vertical recovery by instruments while blind in the clouds. If we had to do it, everyone would be doing it. Sheesh. I'm asking my RIO if he knows about where we are and how high the mountains might be where we currently are soaring. Just as I'm really starting to plan my slow speed recovery, we pop out of the top of the puffy white clouds with blue sky all around us and with our nose pointed almost straight up. As I look around, I see other Phantoms popping out of the clouds with noses pointed up like mushrooms. Whew! My wingman calls "Talley Ho!" What a wonderful feeling of relief! We join up and head back to base and I promise myself... I won't be caught doing that ever again.

Once again, under Lancer's Group Command, we were flying more ACM than any other squadron in the Marine Corps and with no accidents. As a result, the VMFA-112 Cowboys won the Hanson Award as the top Fighter squadron in the Marine Corps which was extremely rare. Reserve Squadrons were typically not honored above the Regular Marine squadrons.

While the Cowboys were getting the improved F-4s, the Air Force was moving from the F-4 Phantom to the McDonnell Douglas F-15 Eagle and the General Dynamics F-16 Falcon. These were newer generation aircraft. The F-15 was a large aircraft, single seat, dual engine fighter and was fairly easy to pick up visually, but it had a superior radar and its power and turn capability were truly impressive. The F-16, on the other hand, was a very small, hard to see, single engine and single seat aircraft. Again it had a superior radar, but with an unmatched turn capability, as it could pull nine G's.

My first encounter with an F-16 was when the Cowboys deployed to Luke Air Force Base in Phoenix, Arizona. I was sent on a mission to fight a single F-16, one versus one. What I soon learned was that the F-16 could always find us on their radar. Then I learned that because they were so small they were very hard to see, even if you knew where to look. Once you got into a visual fight it seemed impossible to beat. It had more power, so it could fight vertically better than the F-4, and it had far superior turning capability so in a horizontal fight you had no chance. The post flight debrief was with a young, Air Force Lieutenant, with just a few hours of flying time, and I was a flyer with over 2,500 hours. It was humiliating, as we had to watch the gun film of him shooting us down.

Over time we learned a few tricks when fighting the F-16. For example, if the F-16 got too slow going straight up, his computer would take control of the aircraft from the pilot. Two versus two we were competitive, but only because we were so experienced. On one hand it was sad to know our aircraft was becoming a dinosaur, but it was also inspiring to know America's next generation of aircraft were so dynamic. A few years later the Navy and Marine Corps began flying the F-18 Hornet. This was a two engine, single seat aircraft with tremendous performance and technology equal if not superior to the Eagle and Falcon.

Before I said goodbye to the Cowboys, I needed to share one more aviator tradition. This could take place anywhere there were lots of pilots and RIOs in one bar such as an Officers Club. While standing around the club drinking and talking with a bunch of separate conversations, someone would call for attention in a serious manner. People stop talking and turn their attention to the speaker. At that point he would yell "Dead Bug!"

Suddenly every person in the bar would drop down to the floor. Chairs would tip over, beers would spill and soon everyone would be lying down on the floor on their backs, with their feet waving up in the air, like a dead bug. Everyone would be looking around because the last person to hit the floor would have to buy the bar a round of drinks. Suddenly everyone would be up and tap dancing as fast as they could and singing, "Anybody who can't tap dance is queer!"

You would look around the bar and everyone had beer stains. Caps were on the floor, chairs were being set back up. The bar would suddenly be different. Everyone was a friend—laughing and clapping each other on the back. The conversations would resume, but now the atmosphere was loose and friendly. Politically correct? Absolutely not, but in the 70's and 80's, political correctness had not yet become the norm. This tradition was called Dead Bug!

Some may feel that I have emphasized the fun and games that were part of my experience too much. But, they were important, and I cherish every memory; and they served a purpose. Part of that stupid fun is to offset the real danger that existed in my flying community. Like most groups that share real danger, the humor is often black. There are not conversations about the possibility of death. To be a fighter pilot means staying calm, cool, and in control of yourself even if you are not in control of every situation. You cannot panic, and you cannot overreact, because it could cause a buddy to die. I also found that fighter crews, regardless of Marine, Navy, or Air Force, had more in common with each other than with crews flying different aircraft such as cargo or bombers from their own service.

During my twenty year career in the Marines and Air Force, I lost over forty friends and acquaintances to flying mishaps. Most jobs don't feature two deaths a year among your peers while on the job. That is a lot of funerals with wives and children.

When people ask me if I miss the flying, I always answer, "Of course I miss the flying. I liked everything about it, and had the opportunity to have unique experiences that I would not trade! But what I miss the most is simply the camaraderie found in a fighter squadron." It is to be treasured!

CHAPTER TWENTY

GENERAL WHITE DINING-IN

Perhaps the evening that is best remembered from my time as the Cowboy's Skipper was a special event that later became known as the General White Dining-In.

During my tour as Skipper, I had a meeting with Fleet and Dog Breath and we decided that we should have a Flight Suit Mess Night, formally known as a Dining-In. I would take the position as President of the Mess, and Fleet and Dog Breath would be the Vice-Presidents of the Mess. Traditionally a Marine Officers Mess or Dining-In is a very structured and formal affair that may careen off into a carnival later in the evening. We made arrangements with the Officer's Club to have a special room prepared.

Thinking it somehow appropriate, I had personally invited Major General Ken Weir, our Commanding General of the 4th Marine Air Wing, to be the guest speaker. To my surprise and pleasure, he said he would come up from New Orleans, the Wing Headquarters, to attend. We were the best squadron in his wing, we had won the coveted Hanson Award, Marine Fighter squadron of the Year, and I guess he wanted to see what we were about.

At a Dining-In you had a Head Table where the Skipper and Executive Officer and Honored Guests would sit, while the rest of the squadron sat at tables positioned perpendicular to the Head Table. The Officers then sat in a specified order so that the senior ranks sat closest to the head table and to the right. If two officers were both of the same rank then they were seated based on date of enrollment in the Marine Corps.

The Head Table is introduced by the Vice President and the squadron stands at attention until the Skipper, "The President", tells them to take their seats. Then a prayer is shared and everyone takes a seat. Typically a Prime Rib Dinner is announced and served.

To that point, the evening had gone pretty much as forecast. Good food, shared camaraderie, sea stories, much drinking: The potential food fight had not gotten into full swing, yet but I could see it coming. At least two rolls had been tossed, which I shushed pretty quickly.

Then the formal events would occur. For a while, various formal toasts were offered and seconded. For example, if a representative from England was present, there will be a toast to the Queen of England. This was accomplished by an Officer standing up and offering a toast. The Vice President would then second the toast and all the Officers would stand and drink the toast. Of course you toast the Group CO, the Wing CO, and the Commandant of the Marine Corps, as well as the United States Marine Corps. Finally a round of Port was served, and when we were ready, the President offered a toast and a minute of silence for fallen comrades.

As you may have gathered, even though food was being served, the Officers in attendance were now really starting to feel their oats. The officers were laughing and conversing and having fun. At the head table Rookie and I were having conversations with Lancer and General Weir.

After a few minutes I felt it was time for me to introduce our honored guest and speaker. It was time for the guest speaker, Gen. Weir to make his remarks. We were all on fairly good behavior, so far. General Weir looked to be enjoying himself.

As I stood up I realized, to my horror, that I couldn't remember our guest's name. Perhaps a toast or two too many. I knew he was a two star general and I believed his name started with a W but I was already standing. I was right beside him so I couldn't now ask someone his name. The entire room was silent and watching. So I forged ahead and said: "It is now my great privilege to introduce our guest of honor and speaker for this evening, Major General... White!"

There is dead silence for a nano second and then one of the Cowboys yells:

"White! You mean General Weir?" The room erupts into yelling, hooting and laughing.

I was so mortified, I put my hand to my head and pretended to faint, falling backward behind the Head Table. I staggered back up and took my seat, General Weir stood up and was laughing.

The Cowboys start chanting, "We want White! We want White!"

General Weir kept laughing and made a joke or two and then gave a tremendous speech. He was a combat veteran and a fighter pilot, so we liked and respected him. He got a standing ovation from the Cowboys.

About then, it was time for the traditional post-meal cigars. Unnoticed by most, two tall lit candles had been placed between the audience and the dais. Suddenly Casino, who had tied a napkin around his head like a samurai warrior, stood up. He then grabbed an Officer's sword that had been brought to the event to give the air of formality to the Dining-In. He walked up to the closest candle, and gave the sword a mighty swing, chopped the candle in two, and caught the top half in his free hand.

He then turned to the rioting crowd and hollered loudly:

"Anybody need a light?"

Then the real food fight started.

The Dining-In was considered a huge success, and my introduction fumble became a legend. General Weir had a great time, and was so gracious that at the end of the evening he presented me with his General Weir name tag for my flight suit. Fleet and Dog Breath and I were very proud of that event.

That Dining-In, although truly a disaster in one sense, is one of my fondest memories. Being in a room with all my brothers and sharing a solemn tradition. Having fun with men I had entrusted my life to while flying is tough to duplicate. Sharing the head table with Lancer, Rookie and General Weir was a special honor. Watching Dog Breath and Fleet coordinate everything in the background made their friendship shine. Being completely surprised and delighted with Casino's hijinks and watching the room erupt with laughter stays with me to this day. For those reasons, I end my tale with a Tribute to the Phantom Fighter Crews with whom I have served.

CHAPTER TWENTY-ONE

FIGHTER TRIBUTE

As I began spending more time with my memories while writing this tale, I started to clearly realize a truth. People don't live forever. Marines don't live forever. In fact, those who fly fighters don't live forever.

Then I began to ponder...if I was gone tomorrow, did I say what I wanted to say to my Marine Brothers? The answer was, "No!"

So I offer this Tribute to them.

When people ask me if I miss the flying, I always say, "Yes, I miss the flying, because when you are flying a Fighter you are totally focused and committed to the fight! It is like nothing else you will ever do (almost). You are totally alive! But to be honest, I miss the squadron and the guys even more than I miss the flying."

"Why?" you might ask.

After all, they were generally a bunch of aggressive, wise-ass, cocky, insulting, sarcastic, bastards in flight suits who thought a funny thing to do was fart and see if they could clear a room. They drank too much, they chased women, they flew when they shouldn't, they laughed too loud, and they thought they owned the skies and every bar they were ever in. They believed they could beat the next guy in whatever they decided to try. Nothing was more funny then screwing with a buddy and seeing how pissed you could get them. They flew aircraft that should have never left the flight line. They flew phantoms that smoked and burnt fuel too fast. They flew aircraft that couldn't turn worth a damn, and sometimes lacked working radars and that featured instruments from decades past.

But a little closer inspection might reveal that every guy in the room was sneaky smart. That they were brutally handsome. They hated to lose and seldom did. They were the laziest guys on the planet until challenged, and then they would do anything to win. They were casually brave. They would fly three feet from their leads' wingtip through the worst night weather, confident that their lead would get them on the ground safely. They would fight ACM until their hearts burst, knowing that the greatest risk was arriving at the six o'clock of a bogey at the same time as their squadron mate.

RIOs were crazy. They would fly with a Phantom pilot at six hundred knots going so low it would have a rooster tail and be blowing over sail boats. They would calmly direct a fight while sitting in an aircraft going straight up with no airspeed, knowing that if the pilot screwed this up, the aircraft would not be recovering. They would remind the pilot in a fight that if they stayed to fight just one minute more in afterburner they would not have the fuel to return and land. They would fly with a pilot doing the most stupid thing they could imagine. On the ground they would call the pilot a dumb shit to his face, then laugh and suit up and go fly with them again the next day. Pilot/RIO teams were created with bonds that would never break.

When we went to another base we assumed we were automatically the best squadron on the base as soon as we landed. We owned any bar we entered (even if it was a no name bar).

We felt we were lucky to have the best pilots, RIOs and Maintenance Troops in the Marine Corps. We found jobs, lost jobs, got married, got divorced, moved, built houses, got rich, got poor, did something stupid and the only thing you could ultimately count on was this. If you really needed something, you would have it from your buddies, without asking.

I miss the Call Signs and the stories behind them. I miss getting lit up at an O' Club full of my buddies, and watching and listening to the incredible, unbelievable things that were happening or being shared. I miss an evil twin brother from Alaska showing up and getting an innocent twin in trouble. I miss squadron Courts and the poor aim of jurors trying to hit the judge. I miss pilots swallowing live roaches. I miss a Mess Night when a candelabra candle could be cut in half with a sword wielding pilot and even General introductions could be screwed up. I miss plane captains saluting as we pull off the flight line. I miss the lighting of the afterburner... especially at night. I miss going straight up and straight down. I miss cross countries and dice games at the bar for drinks. I miss the Octagon. I miss listening to bullshit stories while sharing a drink and laughing till my eyes watered.

I miss three man lifts and the Cowboy choir. I miss Yuma nacho eating contests. I miss naps in the Ready Room, full of buddies scheming up tricks to screw the napping crew. I miss flying upside down in the Grand Canyon. I miss coming into the break hot and looking over and seeing three Phantoms tucked in tight ready to make the boys on the ground proud. I miss belches that could be heard in neighboring states. I miss putting on ad hoc air shows for buddies that may live out on a farm. I miss Sailing Slut cruises.

Finally, I miss hearing "Dead Bug!" being called out and seeing a room full of flyers hitting the deck with chairs and tables tipping over and beers spilling until everyone in the room is lying on their backs in the beer and waving their feet in the air like a dead bug. This being followed closely by everyone in the room tap dancing as fast as they could while yelling "anybody who can't tap dance is queer." That spectacle could not help but make you laugh, slap your buddy on the back and order another round.

I have always been lucky. I have lived a great life and been blessed with a wonderful family and great friends. However, this tribute is to say I know that I was part of something special for many years. I was surrounded by a bunch of talented and crazy guys doing something dangerous and doing it better than most. I got to fly the Phantom. The most brutal, powerful, noisy, but beautiful and solid fighter every built. We were supported by Marines committed and proud to making sure we came home again after every flight. I flew with guys that volunteered to fight America's battles and were willing to die to do it. We had a clear mission and we had fun!

I know that we are lucky bastards to be able to walk into a Ready Room or a bar and have men we respect and love shout out our Call Signs, and know this is truly where we belong. We are United States Marines and we flew the Phantom. We are the Few and the Proud!

I am privileged to call you Brothers! Semper Fi... Shadow

PART EIGHT
Family

CHAPTER TWENTY-TWO

FAMILY

This book is narrowly focused on my life flying and the associated squadron life. But this only tells half the story. While I understand that this chapter of the book may be somewhat redundant, it nevertheless addresses something that was not only vital, but also recognizes the extreme selflessness of the women whose men are in the service. Their sacrifice needs to be recognized.

Susan and I met while in college. We were married when I was in Air Force Pilot Training in Selma, Alabama. I proposed, and she accepted in July of 1969. We were married in October, in Seattle, Washington. We had no honeymoon, as I was required to return to Selma, and resume my training. At first we only had one car, so that made it interesting. We rented a small house that had been turned into a duplex. Our living room and kitchen were separated by the bedroom. The house had no air conditioning, so we bought a huge air plane hangar fan to cool the house. We bought a small puppy and started our married life.

While I was going through training, Susan constantly searched for and worked at different substitute teaching jobs. Gradually she was introduced to the squadron and the wives including my friend Gene and his wife, Sue. They immediately became best friends. Over the next few years we spent time both in North Carolina, living in a small trailer, and in Beaufort, South Carolina, where we lived in an apartment and then base housing. This was a good time, as Susan was introduced into a squadron's social life that included Friday night Happy Hour and Saturday parties. Susan again got a substitute teaching job in Beaufort.

This time also introduced Susan and I to the grim reality that pilots and RIOs died in aircraft accidents. We began attending funerals. A military funeral included a folded American Flag being presented to the widow. A four gun salute was offered followed by the playing of Taps by a single bugler. This was followed by a four plane fly-by over by the squadron aircraft, while in a missing wingman formation. The entire squadron, plus families were in attendance. It was always a powerful ceremony.

When I received my orders to Viet Nam, we decided that Susan would spend a year back up in Seattle with her folks. We drove up to Seattle. A week later she accompanied me to the Seattle Airport with my parents. She kissed me goodbye, and I left for the next twelve months.

For an entire year she lived with her parents. She wrote letters to me every week, and each one had a scent of perfume and her precise writing. The reception of each letter in Viet Nam was a treasured moment. I would lay back in my cot and read a letter from her, and think of home. During that time she also went to school to become a dental assistant.

After six months, I was granted a two week R&R, and so I met Susan in Hawaii. For the next 10 days we enjoyed Oahu and Maui. We laid on the beach, danced, had drinks and enjoyed our time together. However, we both knew that in Viet Nam the massive Project Line Backer, with the bombing of Hanoi, was beginning. That meant that as soon as I got back to the squadron I would be flying over North Viet Nam. The time ended too soon! I returned to Nam Phong, while Susan went back to Seattle.

It is hard for me to know how difficult it was for wives to see their husbands leave to go to war. To write letters knowing that your husband is flying combat missions every day that could end up with him being shot down and becoming a POW, or worse—being killed. In addition to this, the war was very unpopular, and people our age were generally not supportive. That must have been difficult for Susan. Fortunately, both Susan's Dad and my Dad were military veterans, so both families were extremely supportive.

After my Viet Nam tour ended, I arrived back in Seattle. After seeing family and friends, Susan and I spent some private time together, and then we took our two cars and drove down to Mission Viejo, California. We bought our first house. Susan immediately found a job as a Dental Assistant. The squadron had great parties and we visited Monterey, San Diego, San Juan Capistrano and the area. We attended football games at the Rose Bowl, and went skiing in the mountains. We attended concerts and enjoyed the Southern California sun and beaches. We enjoyed the good life. For me it was a tremendous flying adventure for two years. Most importantly, Susan became pregnant just before I received orders to fly with the Air Force in Fort Walton Beach, Florida. So once again she had to quit her job. This time we had a moving transport line move our belongings to Sandy, Florida.

Once there, we bought a small house and began to fit into the Air Force squadron life. We went through Lamaze training and soon she delivered our son, Ty! Again Susan made good friends and we had fun with other couples enjoying boating and the beach. I went on several deployments to Alaska, Hawaii, and Iran while Susan watched the house and our baby.

After Fort Walton Beach, we spent one year in Yuma, Arizona while I began my pursuit of an airline job. We experienced my fiasco with the Airlines, and so together we developed an emergency plan. Susan, Jan, and Ty would go up to a tiny cabin my parents owned in Washington. I would pursue getting a Flight Engineer rating for the Boing 727, and get an Airline Transport Pilot Rating. At the same time I would be applying for more airline jobs, with the search centering on Braniff Airlines and Southwest Airlines, both headquartered in Dallas.

So we separated. Susan, Ty and Jan drove up to Washington, and moved into a tiny, primitive cabin. This was during the Washington rainy season. After three months, I successfully completed both classes and called for Ty and Susan to join me in Dallas. We rented a small apartment. I worked on getting hired by Braniff, and earning a spot in the VMFA-112 Cowboy Marine Reserves squadron.

Once employed by Braniff, we rented another house in Dallas, Texas and decided it was time to add to our family. Susan soon got pregnant. We decided to build a house in Flower Mound, Texas. It would be on an acre lot in the rolling hills North of Dallas. We would include a Mother-In-Law Suite. It would be special. The house took one year to build. It was beautiful. Susan delivered our beautiful baby girl, Samantha. We had a great little family and a beautiful new home and a terrific job. I was flying with the Marine Reserves. Life was good!

By that time Susan had lived in twelve different houses in ten states. She had been asked to make new friends multiple times and to find multiple temporary jobs. She had delivered and began raising two children. She had attended multiple funerals. She had stayed at home or lived with her parents while I flew combat missions and went on multiple deployments. My point again is to emphasize that sacrifice is made by wives that must be recognized.

We lived in our new house for two months. On July 4, 1978 I was told I was furloughed from Braniff. Braniff had made the largest furlough of pilots in airline history. Susan and I lay in our bed, in our new master bedroom, and looked at the ceiling and wondered what we were to do now. We had no savings. We had two kids. We had a big house payment and I was too old for most airlines (31).

In desperation, my friend Dog Breath helped me develop a resume. I applied to jobs involving sales, medicine and/or computer technology. I was very lucky! After two months I was hired by a company that provided computer information systems to hospitals. I knew nothing about computers, sales or hospitals. Sheesh! I worked in that field for the next twenty five years.

Over the next eight years I chased promotions within different companies in the Hospital Information System field. During that time, we moved west to Los Angeles, north to Seattle, and then east to Chicago.

I continued to commute to Dallas from those different locations each month, and continued flying with the Cowboys . Unfortunately, because Susan was always across the country, she was no longer part of the squadron life. The single exception was when she came to the ceremony when I became Commanding Officer. I retired from the Reserves in 1988, as a Lieutenant Colonel.

Was our experience unusual? Perhaps, on the other hand, some things were common and shared by all the pilot and RIO wives. Months, if not years, of separation and weekends alone with the children. The knowledge that your husband was doing very dangerous work and death could come with the job. Knowing that your husband had a passion for flying and the squadron life, which you could only share at a distance.

The wives I knew were typically strong, intelligent, attractive, loyal and supportive of their husband's other passion in life. They met women across the country and made friendships that still live today. They enjoyed being a part of squadron life. They took fierce pride in their man's service to the country and were proud of both their career and success.

So, this book is primarily focused on flying the Phantom and introducing the adventures and escapades of the men with whom I shared this life. However, it only tells half the story. For that I apologize. Please understand, that it would not have been possible or enjoyable without the loving support of Susan.

Thank you Susan!

EXTERIOR HOOCH ROSE GARDEN

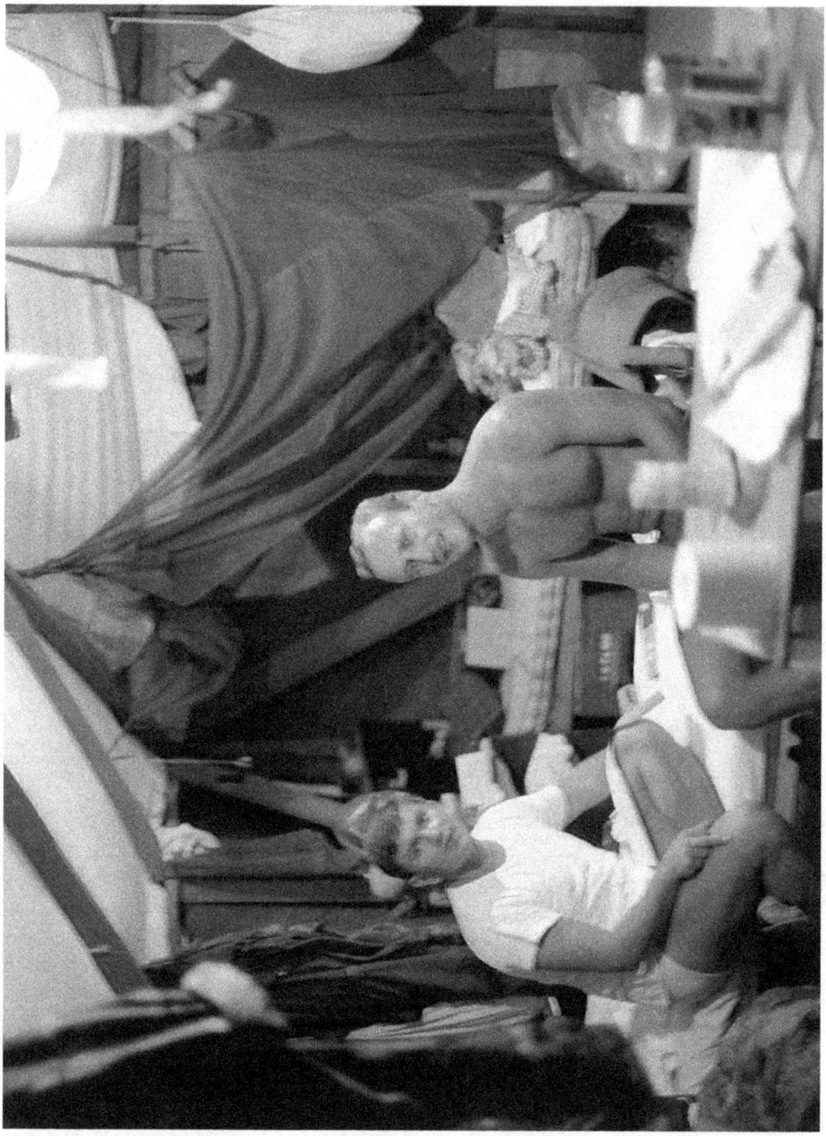

INTERIOR HOOCH ROSE GARDEN

DEVIL MAINTENANCE ROSE GARDEN

GROUND FIRE BATTLE DAMAGE

BOB HOPE SHOW ROSE GARDEN

HAVE IDEA MIG-21

HAVE IDEA PHANTOM AND 2 MIG-21s

SNAKES HAVE IDEA

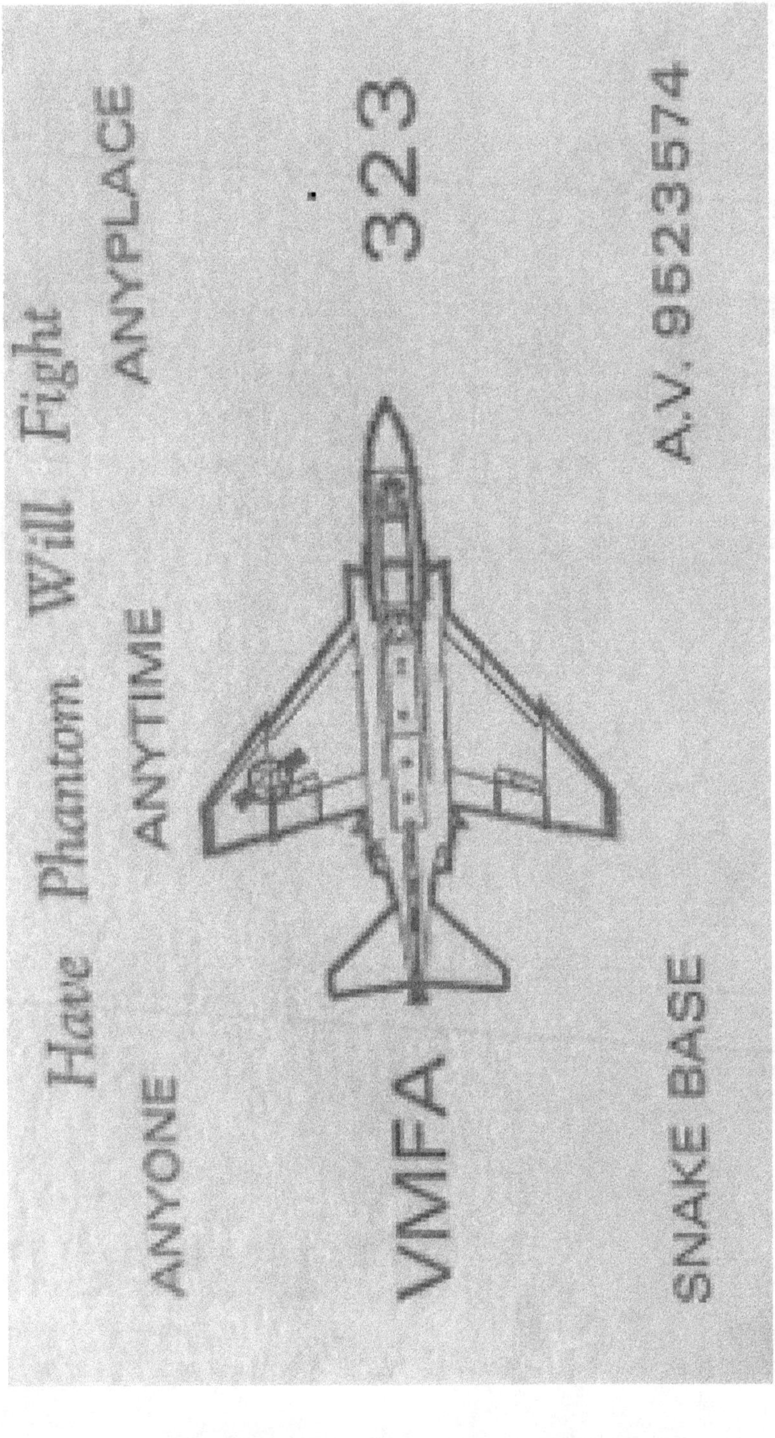
Have Phantom Will Fight
ANYONE ANYTIME ANYPLACE
VMFA 323
SNAKE BASE A.V. 9523574

LION AIR FORCE F-4E

COWBOY DEPLOYMENT

Printed in the USA
CPSIA information can be obtained
at www.ICGtesting.com
LVHW091403121223
766083LV00053B/1171

9 780974 541471